SHRED GIRLS

LINDSAY'S JOYRIDE

MOLLY HURFORD

ILLUSTRATED BY VIOLET LEMAY

RODALE
KiDS

Text copyright © 2019 by Molly Hurford
Cover art and interior illustrations copyright © 2019 by Violet Lemay

All rights reserved. Published in the United States by Rodale Kids, an imprint of Random House Children's Books, a division of Penguin Random House LLC, New York. Originally self-published in paperback and in slightly different form in 2017.

Rodale and the colophon are registered trademarks and Rodale Kids is a trademark of Penguin Random House LLC.

Visit us on the Web! rhcbooks.com

Educators and librarians, for a variety of teaching tools, visit us at RHTeachersLibrarians.com

Library of Congress Cataloging-in-Publication Data is available upon request.
ISBN 978-1-63565-277-2 (hc) — ISBN 978-1-9848-9425-0 (lib. bdg.) — ISBN 978-1-63565-278-9 (ebook)

Printed in the United States of America
10 9 8 7 6 5 4 3 2 1
2019 Rodale Kids Edition

⇒ Training Log ⇐

For as long as I can remember, I've lived in a world that's full of superheroes.

At least that's what my parents say when they complain about the comic books all over the house, or all the posters in my room, or the times that I'm watching cartoons instead of doing homework. I try to explain that I'm not "wasting time" or "killing brain cells," as they call it.

I'm researching. And this summer I'm logging all my research here, in my guide to being a superhero.

I figure I'm super qualified to be super (ha-ha, get it?), since I have my own strict training regimen. Not every wannabe superhero bothers with that. See, every day I come home from school and do the same thing:

3:30 p.m.–4:00 p.m.: Research via watching cartoons while eating a (healthy) snack.

4:00 p.m.–4:15 p.m.: Intelligence gathering, i.e., skimming Mom's morning newspaper for any recent heists.

4:15 p.m.–4:45 p.m.: Daily report. I take the info I just got from the newspaper plus the notes that I thought of during my earlier research and put them into this journal so I can reference them later.

4:45 p.m.–5:00 p.m.: Stretching using the yoga mat Mom has set up in the living room. Even in the Justice League, I know they do warm-ups before training, which leads to . . .

5:00 p.m.–6:00 p.m.: Intensive physical training. Can be done outside on the tire-and-ladder obstacle course my dad helped me build, or in my basement crime-fighting training center . . . which is really just a crime-in-progress scene with a bunch of my villainous teddy bears and old dolls set up as targets. But Mom promised this year I could get a punching bag for my birthday, so the countdown is on.

6:00 p.m.: Dinnertime and back to my alter ego, plain old Lindsay.

With all this training, how could I not be destined to be a superhero?

Also, I'm pretty sure my cousin Phoebe is a supervillain, so I have a built-in archnemesis.

Okay, I admit, it's a little unlikely that she's an actual super-villain. But I need to start somewhere and I like a good project. From my research, an epic battle is pretty key in the superhero game. I mean, anyone can do good, but to take it to the next level, it seems like superheroes always need to have a "big bad" to fight. And it's so easy to want to fight with supervillain Phoebe. She wears all black, dyes her dark hair crazy colors, pierced her entire ear when she was eighteen—and then got a bunch of tattoos. She's been adding to her tattoo collection since then, and now that she's twenty-three, she's living on her own in an apartment a few miles from her parents' house and my house, and her style has only gotten wilder over the years.

I have to confess, I secretly think she looks kind of cool (in a villainous way), but her attitude really isn't very cool at all. . . . Usually she just ignores me, and I've heard her yelling at her mom in the kitchen while we're over there for dinner. The stereo in her old room at her parents' house—even with the door slammed shut—actually seemed to pulse the walls and floors, and when she brought friends by, they looked like they could have been rejected by the Legion of Doom for being too obvious.

Like today, I walked down to the kitchen to get a snack—a superhero-in-training needs to keep her strength up—and I heard my mom on video chat with my aunt, and Tía Maria was complaining for the millionth time about something Phoebe was up to now that she's moved into her own apartment. I think she got into trouble at school or work or something, maybe. . . . Whatever it was,

Tía Maria was shrieking that Phoebe was going to get hurt if she kept up what she'd been doing, no amount of training could protect her, and why couldn't she be more like Tía was when she was her age? (Between you and me, I've seen the photo albums, and the way Tía Maria dressed when she was younger wasn't exactly a style I'd want either. Shoulder pads and enormous hair, yikes.)

But anyway, Phoebe definitely stands out. She spends family parties mostly ignoring me and listening to music with her headphones on. Okay, that may not be a major indicator that she's a supervillain, but I need to start somewhere when it comes to finding an archnemesis.

(Hey, I didn't make the rules. I just read about them.)

Superhero Tip: All good superheroes have an archnemesis. You can still be an equal-opportunity crime fighter and stop all crimes, but your main focus always needs to be thwarting your archnemesis. Otherwise, there's no way your comic book will become a well-known series. Obviously.

Before you roll your eyes, just hear me out. You're probably my age, and you might be someone who would be my best friend in school. (Maybe. Actually, I'm pretty shy in real life.) Or you might ignore me and laugh at me with your friends at the lunch table. But you know what? I bet you've also thought about how cool it would be if life were a little more like your Saturday-morning cartoons.

(And if you don't think being able to jump into other dimensions or fly would be cool, maybe we wouldn't be best friends after all.)

I know it sounds crazy, but I really believe that I could be a superhero. The world may not be under imminent threat of alien invasion yet, but if it happens, wouldn't it be great if there was someone around prepared to deal with it?

Lately, I started using my Wonder Woman notebook (I'm writing in it right now!) to take notes on everything I see or read that may come in handy one day—like when Catwoman says that to disarm a bomb you don't need to worry about which wire is blue or red and you can just cut them all. (I know she's a bad guy, but it seems like good advice.)

I've also been trying to sketch out some of the cooler fight scenes so I can practice them later. I've tried to get good enough to do a front kick so high that it goes over my head, but I think that might be a skill specific to cartoons, not real life.

Still, that will always be the dream, along with having bright red hair like Batgirl.

My mom says that women in the stuff I read and watch are bad role models for me, because they promote an "unhealthy body image." But I told her that at least I don't want to be like Barbie, whose dimensions are so unrealistic they're almost inhuman, so she backed off a little. I still see her muttering when I'm watching cartoons sometimes, though. Mom's really into being a feminist. She told me that back in college, when she would write about how movies and books needed more female heroines, she didn't mean women who wore teensy skirts and high-heeled boots to save the world. And now that she's a cultural anthropologist, she's always trying to get me to read about women from ancient civilizations and matriarchal cultures—those are cultures where women are in charge. Some of the stuff she gives me to read is actually pretty cool (but don't tell her I said that).

I keep telling her that I've been working on a design for a costume that would be the most effective, which doesn't include heels or a short skirt. I've paid attention: short skirts get ripped, no live-action female hero can run in heels, capes get grabbed, and covering up is just a good safety measure. It's probably best to wear something like Catwoman's and Batgirl's full-sleeve jumpsuits, though without Batgirl's cape. Of course, I'm thinking it also needs to be something that wouldn't stand out too much in a crowd—I don't want to do a Superman and wear it under my clothes all the time. That would get way too hot in the summer. I'm trying to be practical.

But last time I tried to make a costume, it didn't go so well. I had it perfectly planned out: an outfit that would let me fly over fences and leap tall buildings in a single bound—or at least jump off the top of the slide we have in the backyard without tearing anything or showing the world my underwear. My sewing abilities, though, are far from super.

I may have cut my jeans a little on the short side—but at least I put my purple tights under them so I wouldn't run the risk of scraping my legs on fences as I vaulted over! And looking back, that old glittery leotard from my one disastrous attempt at gymnastics class wasn't the best choice for a top. It was a little beat-up-looking, and there's a chance that Mom was right and I had outgrown it a couple of years ago. It did feel a little strained at the seams when I put it on. Mom took one look at me and said there was no way I was even going outside in that outfit and I looked like a "street urchin." (Yeah, I don't know what that means either.)

The next day, when I was emptying the trash cans while doing my chores, I spotted my poor cutoffs at the bottom of the trash can in the kitchen, so Mom won that round.

Okay, I've probably said too much—I'll use up this whole diary in a week if I'm not careful. But I don't really have anyone to talk to about this stuff at school. I have friends and everything, but I don't talk about the whole "superhero quest" stuff—like I said before, I know it sounds kind of out there. And being twelve is difficult enough without having everyone in my class thinking I'm nuts, or perpetually yelling "It's a bird, it's a plane, it's . . . Lindsay!" every time I walk past them. (You laugh now, but when it happens, it's not so funny.) So I keep my secret identity under wraps, which is just Superhero 101 anyway.

Superhero Tip: A superhero needs to have an alter ego: Superman's is Clark Kent, Batman's is Bruce Wayne, and mine is . . . me. It helps if you can wear glasses like Superman does when he's in disguise—as Clark Kent, he looks too nerdy to be saving the world.

So far I have the nerdy part covered: every time I walk down the hall at school or try to blend in at the mall, I know I'm not fooling anyone into thinking I'm cool. (I guess on the bright side, I have the perfect Clark Kent–style mild-mannered disguise. Too bad I don't have an alter ego to match Superman. Yet.)

When I look in the mirror, I don't see anything super: just a pointy chin, more muscle than I'd like, and definitely, completely, unlike the skinny blond girls at school. I'm no Batgirl, that's for sure. I would love to call my hair wavy and chestnut, but really it's just kind of poofy and mouse brown, and long enough to be that boring in-between length. And like Clark Kent, I wear wire-rimmed glasses—which the lady at LensCrafters assured my mom were back in style. (She whispered it, really, but I heard. Maybe I have super hearing too? Either way, I got the glasses. I don't love them.)

But deep down I know that the superhero side of me is just one spider bite or lightning strike away, and I'll be ready for it. So I'm going to keep this log running for the summer, now that school is out. The first priority is coming up with a witty sign-off. I'm having a bit of writer's block at the moment, but I'm sure something will come to me.

> Brilliantly yours,
> Lindsay
> (That's not it.)

Training Log

I should back up and add that my parents are pretty cool. I shouldn't say that they're unsupportive of my superhero goals. They're both cultural anthropologists—that's how they met, studying in college—and according to my research, it's a pretty good profession for a superhero's parents to have. I figure they'll eventually stumble on some kind of magic artifact on a dig somewhere, bring it home as a trophy, and then bam! Superpowers for all of us.

The only problem I have with Mom and Dad is . . . well, that there isn't any problem. How can I ever become a superhero without some kind of great tragedy or huge obstacle to overcome? I know what you're thinking: that I'm a terrible daughter. Well, I'm not. It's not like I want to be in a Batman scenario—parents shot in an alley after an opera, their killer never caught, swearing vengeance, et cetera.

For one thing, we don't go to operas. For another, we don't have a butler who could raise me and help me become Batman. Also, I know I'd miss them, and I don't think I have the personality to be as brooding and mysterious as a Batman-type superhero.

So I'm counting on the magical artifact, which I'm hoping will happen any day now.

Forever flying,

Lindsay

(Absolutely not.)

CHAPTER 1

It's hard to believe that it's finally summer break for us. . . . It's so weird to just have the whole day stretching out ahead of me and nothing really going on, except for thinking about new ways to beat a bad guy in a fight. The free time—and the summer heat—are great, but in some ways I'm already missing school. This morning birds were chirping and the sun was beaming when I woke up, and immediately when I walked down to get breakfast, Mom was pestering me to get outside and play. That's when I remembered the worst part about summer break: my parents trying to make me spend the whole day running around outside. So we compromised over breakfast: I would walk outside, but to my favorite spot.

And now, as I walk down the block toward the library to trade out some comic books, my mind wanders to why exactly I can't be a superhero. My parents say that I have a problem accepting reality—they even sent me to a therapist once when I was nine! (Okay, so it was because I tried to fly off the top of my swing set. It didn't work, by the way, but how else was I supposed to try out the Hawkgirl wings that I made?)

The therapist understood, though. She told my parents that there wasn't anything wrong with me, that I was just "creative" and "imaginative." She didn't think that there was a problem, so they eased up a little. Since then they've tried to be supportive, sending me to comic book drawing classes and taking me to comic conventions. They once even dressed up like Clark Kent's parents and got me a Supergirl costume. I'd like to say it was awesome, but to be honest, it was pretty embarrassing. They kept taking pictures with every Superman they saw and wouldn't get out of character!

I'm actually amazed, as I walk down the street completely, wonderfully alone, that they even let me out of the house to do errands like this. That's a new thing this summer: when school ended, my parents still had to work during the day, but they said I'm old enough to stay home alone, and even walk to the library, as long as that's the only place I go. They can be pretty strict: I still have a bedtime, and there's no going out with boys (not that any boys in my class are that cute anyway) or hanging out at the mall without adult supervision—the classic parent stuff. I usually don't mind too much. With all my superhero training, I don't have a lot of time to hang out anyway. But being able to walk alone to the library is already my favorite hobby of the summer—so every step I take has a little more bounce in it.

As I round the last corner, I catch my reflection in a store window. Alley23 is right next to the library, and my mom does not approve of the clothing sold there, so I've never actually gone in. But that doesn't stop me from pausing to dream about going in one day. For the last month they've displayed an ideal Catwoman–meets–Supergirl black jumpsuit in the front window. Without my mom, I can finally take a good look at it, so . . . I do. On the mannequin, it's not skintight like Catwoman's normal uniform: it's got a wide neck and three-quarter-length sleeves, and the top and bottom are divided by a light gray band. The top is tighter, but the bottom is almost like harem pants instead of leggings, and close up it's not actually all black—it's navy blue, almost inky-looking. It's a silky, shimmering fabric, and I can imagine myself doing a sweet flying kick wearing it.

I see my reflection over the mannequin, and it almost looks like I'm wearing this jumpsuit, and I envision show-ing up at school and looking like I run the place. I know it would be just my style—if I were allowed to have a style anyway. See, I got lucky for a superhero-in-training. I know I worked for it, but without too much effort, my biceps are already looking extra tough. I wouldn't mess with me. My mom says I got that from her side of the family—all the ladies have muscles to spare. They also tend to have that glam, curvaceous thing going for them . . . and as far as I can tell, it's skipped me altogether. I'm less va-va-voom and more comic book BOOM at best. I'd say I'm still twelve and maybe I'll have a "glow-up" in a few years, but most of the girls in my grade are fully "glowed" already. I'm still flat as a board. I'm just a board with biceps. But that's fine—it's just more proof that I was destined to be a superhero. A superhero who should probably own this jumpsuit.

But when it comes to my wardrobe, it's like my parents are actively preventing me from dressing anything like a superhero, or even their alter egos. No catsuits here. And Alley23 isn't just jumpsuits—it's full of cool leggings and bright sleeveless tank tops, while I'm stuck in a too-baggy T-shirt and too-long jean shorts that make me look about nine years old. I'm pretty sure that if Mom had it her way, I'd be wearing the same exact jumpers that I wore when I was seven, with matching Peter Pan–collar shirts. Yuck. (And who still wears those anyway? I don't even know where she buys stuff like that anymore.)

And why am I complaining about all of that? Because of my archnemesis, of course—the Joker to my Batman: my cousin Phoebe. (Insert dramatic music here.) She couldn't be more different from me if she tried. And I bet she would buy that jumpsuit.

Archnemeses are hard to find, and from a comic book standpoint, she seems like my perfect opposite. She even looks a little like Catwoman

in one of the books I'm just about to return: muscular like me, but that "curvy gene" didn't skip her part of the generation. And while she looks a lot like her mom with her dark hair and big, dark eyes, Phoebe's short-cropped hair is spiked up, and her tattoos poke out of her sleeves even when she's trying to cover them up.

Come to think of it, since my aunt is my mom's sister, Phoebe probably had the same rules as me growing up. Maybe Tía Maria was even stricter, since she's older than my mom.

Yeesh. No wonder Phoebe became a supervillain. I mean, what choice did she have?

With a sigh, I take one last look at that perfect jumpsuit before walking into the library next door. I just know I'd be a superhero if I were allowed to wear it. Maybe Phoebe has it right; even I'd consider a life of crime if it meant ditching my pink shirts for a better wardrobe.

But I can't be bummed for long. Walking into our small-town library, I feel instantly at home. The smell of old books mixed with new ones comes over me as Karen, the cool, younger librarian, greets me with a nod and a quiet "Hi there, Lindsay." It's one of the only places that I feel completely comfortable, and now that the librarian knows that I'm into comic books, she's been making sure they get all the new ones.

She waves me over to the counter. "Got the latest

Batman and stashed it back here for you," she says, reaching under the counter and pulling it out.

"Thanks!" I say enthusiastically. "I've been dying to read this one."

"I know. Enjoy!" She winks and turns around to help another person, and I head to the best part of the library: the section for the comics and graphic novels is tucked away in a corner, where a couple of beanbag chairs have recently been added. I sink into my favorite one, flip open my new comic, and settle in for an afternoon of reading and studying. (Who knew there were so many ways to do a flying kick?)

The day flies by as I'm reading—Karen even brought me a pile of other comic books she thought I'd love, and I'm just about to dive into a Wonder Woman comic that I've never seen before when I feel a presence looming, and a shadow falls over my reading light.

Trust the popular girls to ruin a good book. My blissful afternoon is rudely interrupted as Dana walks by. Remember the skinny blond girls from school who don't look like me? Dana is sort of their leader.

She doesn't look happy to be there, and while I've never really talked to her in school, I can't imagine why she's here instead of hanging out with her friends at the local pool. She's more dressed for that, in tiny, artistically ripped jean shorts with a pink tank top, her blond hair even lighter than it was during the school year, but just as perfectly straightened. She looks like she stepped off the pages of *Generically Cool Preteen Magazine*. (Do I sound jealous or catty?)

While she doesn't actually say anything to me—she never does, so this isn't a shock—she does look me up and down, and after her eyes fall on the Wonder Woman comic that I'm holding, she tosses her hair and walks toward the Young Adult section, bypassing graphic novels. I can practically see her thinking, *What baby still reads comic books?*

I feel like screaming after her, "Adults read comic books too! Also, who actually tosses their hair in real life?"

Of course, I don't. But wouldn't it be cool if I did?

I know I should get back to my reading—the library closes in a couple of hours, and I have so much more work to do!—but I keep an eye trained on her to see what she ends up picking to read. Then I almost fall off my beanbag when Karen greets her by name, like she did with me, and hands her a book from behind the desk. Dana thanks her and walks out—but on her way out the door, we lock eyes (superhero tip: seriously, get better at watching someone out of the corner of your eye!). She gives me a small smile and an even smaller nod.

Huh. That was more pleasant than I expected. My superhero brain takes over, and I start imagining what it would have been like if I'd been bolder, gone up and said hello or asked what she was reading. I want to do some detective work and ask Karen what Dana was reading, but I feel like that might be sort of weird. So instead I go back to my books for a while longer before packing up and starting the walk home to make it back for dinner. This might be the one part of the day I'm most excited for, since Mom promised to make her famous enchiladas (with her secret sauce).

⋙ Training Log ⋘

When I came home from the library with a stack of books, I thought Mom would be annoyed that every single one of them was a comic, but she seemed distracted. She even let me have a soda, although it was already after five p.m. You know how when something big is about to happen, it sometimes seems . . . quiet? That's how this afternoon has felt. I'm on red alert, feeling really jumpy. . . . Or maybe I can't handle caffeine this late in the day!

> **Superhero Tip:** No overdoing it on the caffeine. You always want to be in control of your hands. Mine get way too shaky.

Queasily yours,
Lindsay
(Definitely not.)

CHAPTER 2

Summer vacation started earlier this week, and it turns out I wasn't just being dramatic in my journal. (It's happened before.) But this time something big really is about to happen. My parents come into my room while I work on turning a swimsuit into the bottom part of a costume. Mom sighs when she sees it, but for once she doesn't bug me about it. That's a pretty good indication that something's up.

She and Dad sit down on the bed, and I can just tell—I can feel it in my gut—that this is the start of my epic adventures. They don't say anything, and it makes me nervous, until I realize that they're both smiling.

Big relief. Despite kind of wanting some kind of tragic element in my life—you know, to better fight crime—I'm not really ready for anything truly tragic to happen.

Mom takes a deep breath. "We need to talk."

(Never mind. This might be bad after all.)

Dad laughs at my expression. "Nothing bad, kiddo," he quickly adds, and my mom smiles.

Phew.

"You remember that dig we were trying to get involved with in Estonia?" she asks.

"Yes . . . ," I answer, trying to act much calmer than

I feel. This is it! The dig where I "accidentally" get lost, stumble on a magic artifact, and gain the superpowers I've been waiting for.

"Well, we got invited!" My dad grins.

"That's awesome!" I jump up to hug both of them. "When do we leave?"

When their faces fall, I know in my gut—this is the truly tragic moment of my life. I'm not going.

"Sweetie, we'd love to have you, but actually we think it'd be better for you to stay here—" my mom says.

"—with your cousin Phoebe!" Dad enthuses. "You're going to stay with her at her new apartment near Tía Maria's for a few weeks this summer. You're going to have so much fun!"

They both look so proud of themselves, but all I can do is smile weakly back at them.

Crud.

Why would Phoebe want me to stay with her? My immediate thought is that she wants to convert me to her evil ways before my powers start working—that way, I'm already on the dark side. And in a weird sense, I can see why Phoebe might want me to turn into her. Mom is always saying that Phoebe and I look alike, so maybe she wants a mini-me version of herself. We have the same eyes and nose, and the same boring brown hair—and like me, Phoebe has always been muscular.

Even I have to admit we kind of look like sisters, or

twins separated by a tragic time machine accident. Well, we used to anyway. Now she has probably ten holes in each ear, filled with weird earrings (clearly part of her supervillain costume—some of them were skulls). We might have the same eyes still, but you can't really tell, since every time you see Phoebe she wears a ton of dark eye makeup. I think it looks really cool, but I know my mom and my aunt hate it. (Dark makeup is a supervillain thing and all, but I still wish I could at least try it on sometime.)

"Lindsay?" my dad says, looking concerned.

Darn. I zoned out and into my own imagination again.

"I heard you," I respond dully. But the shock is still settling in.

I mean, as soon as Phoebe moved out of her parents' house, she cut her hair into short spikes, and every time I see her, her naturally dark hair has streaks of a different color mixed in: red, green, blue, purple. Once, it was even bright white!

Phoebe also has a lot of tattoos, which caused a lot more grumpy phone calls from her mom to mine. (They aren't exactly quiet talkers.) She started getting them as soon as she went to college, and I was fascinated when she would come home covered in more and more colors and pictures. I hadn't realized she would be my archnemesis one day, so at the time, I thought it was kind of cool. She has a massive tattoo on her back of a tree and a bunch of branches surrounded by all types of birds: there are gulls and small birds flying, sparrows perched on branches, an owl blinking near the top of the tree, and a weird variety of birds that can't fly walking around down by the roots—a penguin, an ostrich, and a dodo!

I know it's probably an evil penguin, but it is my favorite. I love the way it looks like it's about to waddle away—it's so lifelike. She also has words written on her ribs, and a bunch of other smaller tattoos that I only catch glimpses of when she's over. I've never gotten close enough to read them. I'm sure there's some kind of evil power or meaning behind them, but just between you and me, I still think they look pretty cool. My mom tells me that I'm never ever allowed to get tattoos, especially after we see Phoebe at family parties, when a couple of the grandmothers start telling her she doesn't look proper, crossing themselves and whispering. (My great-aunt really likes her tattoos, though, and she keeps the family from complaining too much.)

Phoebe's supervillain costume might look cool, but it's pretty impractical. She's always wearing a lot of jewelry, and her ripped jeans would definitely get caught on something midfight.

My mom must have registered that something about their Estonia plan wasn't exactly thrilling me, because her smile fades and she looks more concerned. "I know it's a long time to be away from home," she says. "But your dad and I, and your aunt and uncle, all think that Phoebe could be really great for you to spend time with, and they'll be nearby. And Phoebe's excited about it too—I promise."

Despite her supervillain style, my parents still love Phoebe a lot. She got straight As all through school and she's in a graduate program now (supervillains are just as smart as superheroes—that's why they're "super"), and she comes home to see her family on weekends, even though at twenty-three she's old enough that she doesn't technically have to. I heard my mom tell my dad how sweet it is that Phoebe trains with my uncle on the weekends, which surprised me a lot: it must mean that my uncle is in on the supervillain thing. Mom and Dad love Phoebe, and while they don't love how she looks, they constantly try to get me to talk to her about college and school and stuff.

So I guess that's what they're up to, putting us together for the summer, and since I kind of am hoping that (a) I can defeat Phoebe as my first superhero act, and (b) my parents might find a superpower-infested artifact and bring it home as a present for me, I don't want to burst into tears or tell them to stay home.

"I'm just going to miss you guys," I say, sniffling a bit.

And of course, that's when Mom starts crying and even Dad gets a bit misty-eyed. Naturally, they both pull me in for a massive group hug—my family is big on the hugging—and I feel a little better, even if I'm slightly squished and my prized stuffed rabbit, Mr. Muffin, is stuck under all of us, completely squashed. Once Mom starts crying, though, it's almost easier for me to pull myself together—I mean, one of us has to be mature, right?

Besides, a plan is starting to form in my head. I'm imagining them coming home to their newly grown-up and superpowered daughter, being incredibly proud of me. Of course, I don't think anyone else in my family realizes that Phoebe's a supervillain, so I can't explain why I would never follow in her footsteps like they seem to want me to. So I'm hoping that she and I can battle it out as superpeople, and then once I defeat her and make her see the light, our normal-people alter egos can go back to being friends at family dinners. We haven't talked much since she went to the dark side.

Training Log

What does someone pack to go stay with a supervillain? You would think TV would have prepared me for this.

Now that I'm packing up and preparing for battle, I don't know how much time I'll have to write. I'll try to keep you updated as best I can.

> **Superhero Tip:** No matter how super you are, packing enough clean underwear is still a top priority.

Live long and prosper,
Lindsay
(No, I stole that one.)

CHAPTER 3

As I'm packing the day before Phoebe comes to take me away, I'm still unsure of what to bring. It'll be a few weeks of living with her, and I've never been away from home that long. I'm not sure how many pairs of underwear to bring. I'm not sure if Mr. Muffin should come along or if that will give Phoebe leverage to hold him hostage (or just make fun of me). I don't know if I should pack comic books, or if that will make my duffel bag too heavy. And I don't know if I should bring old favorites or new ones I haven't read. That's somehow the hardest decision I've faced so far: new books that I may or may not like, or old ones that I know I'll love rereading but might get a little tired of by the end of two months.

Clothes are easy, though. I don't really have many to choose from, and they're all pretty much chosen by Mom on our annual school shopping trip anyway. Jeans that are a little too loose to be skinny, a little too tight to be considered baggy in a stylish way. T-shirts that are about the same—not cool, not uncool, just . . . shirts. Some of them have comic book characters on them, but getting those is a hard-fought battle, since Mom is encouraging me to be "trendy," whatever that means. (And I don't think it means what she thinks it means.)

Take the last time we went shopping, for example. We were getting clothes for this spring, since I've outgrown most of my stuff. I told Mom I wanted to wear more funky patterns and have more of a cool-librarian style. You know, clothes that Batgirl would wear on her days off. But Mom had other ideas, mainly pinks and plaids—and I really hate those.

So we ended up at the mall, with Mom pulling clothes off the kid racks while I tried to slip into the junior section. We barely made it out alive, and there wasn't even a villain to fight or a science experiment that went horribly wrong and attacked the mall.

The biggest fight came when I was trying on a maroon miniskirt with a mustard-yellow sweater in the dressing room, and as soon as I opened the door, before she even got a good look at it, Mom was shaking her head and saying, "Absolutely not." And then she held up a knee-length light pink skirt and said it was a lot more "appropriate" for someone my age.

Someone my age who has never been to a public school maybe. But if I walked into school wearing that droopy pink nightmare, I'd look even more out of place than I do already.

We ended up compromising on a pair of jeans, eating a pretzel together, and both coming home grumpy.

And now, by the time I finish packing, my big duffel bag is jammed and I'm struggling with the zipper when

I hear Mom's footsteps on the stairs. I'm hoping that she won't ask to see what I've packed, since I've left out almost every pink thing I own—all the stuff she bought me, basically—and I've kept in as many T-shirts as I could, plus my more comfortable jeans and jean shorts.

I hear Mom's telltale double knock at the door and know she's about to come in. I leap at my duffel bag and just yank the zipper shut as fast as I can. There's no point in packing a secret wardrobe if it's not so secret anymore.

Sure enough, Mom comes in. She peers around, knowing something happened but not able to put her finger on exactly what. I can see her face readjust as she decides to focus on what she came to say. "You know, Linds, we're not just hoping that you'll have a fun time with your cousin—we're hoping you'll learn a bunch from her too," she says.

I'm shocked. Does Mom really think I'm going to take on Phoebe's supervillain tendencies after just one summer? I can't imagine Mom being thrilled if I come back covered in black eyeliner, listening to angry music and planning a museum heist. I nod stiffly anyway, because this isn't really a topic I want to discuss.

"I can't believe I'm not going to see you for so long," she says, and I can see that she's tearing up again, which makes me swallow a little harder. "You're so grown up!"

"I know, I know," I mumble. "At least you never sent me to summer camp before." (I mean, that sounds like the absolute worst. There aren't libraries at those camps, only craft rooms!)

"We'll call a lot," she says tearfully, and gives me a hug. "But promise you'll try to make a couple of new friends while you're with Phoebe?"

I nod again, but my fingers are crossed behind my back. Mom seems happy with that response, though, and after pulling out a couple of pink shirts ("I think you forgot to pack this one! And this one!"), she leaves me in the quiet of my room.

Mr. Muffin is the last thing to get slipped into my duffel, so he won't get cramped in my big bag. Knowing he's in there makes where I'm going feel a little less scary, potential hostage or not.

I take one last, longing look around my room, which seems strangely empty now that I've finished packing. All the comic books in the world couldn't make this summer good for me. My duffel bag feels way too heavy, and I almost trip as I'm heading downstairs. That would be great—start the summer with my archnemesis while on crutches thanks to a stair-induced sprained ankle.

But I make it down unscathed and sink onto the couch clutching my book, wishing that the summer were already over.

≋ Training Log ≋

This morning is officially go time. Phoebe's supposed to be here at noon today to pick me up to take me to her apartment, just twenty minutes from here across town, and I'm going to be ready for her. I've been reading up on mind-control techniques and how to block them, so no matter what kind of mind control she thinks she's going to try, I've got it covered. I even started meditating, because apparently, the clearer your mind is, the stronger it is, and the easier it should be to resist the dark side. Or that's my current theory anyway. I thought about working more on my roundhouse kicks, but I figured Phoebe's not likely to start a battle with me immediately: she doesn't know I'm onto her, so I'm going to use the element of surprise and catch her in the act of . . . well, whatever evil thing she's planning. The important part is that she doesn't know I know.

> **Superhero Tip:** Act casual. You don't want your arch-nemesis to know you're onto her. Better to infiltrate her evil organization and figure out exactly what she's up to. Plus, if I'm stuck with Phoebe all summer, I don't want things to be weird right away.

Stay golden,
Lindsay
(Hate it.)

CHAPTER 4

I made a couple of packing changes last night after my first attempt: I decided to bring my favorite comic books and DVDs instead of the new ones, and some extra super-hero workout gear (like my favorite Superman T-shirt and shorts). And now I'm sitting in my room, reviewing fight scenes to prepare for Phoebe's arrival, when I hear a car coming up the driveway. I look out the window and see a giant black van with a huge skull airbrushed on the side. Seriously? She's coming to pick me up in her supervillain-mobile? What will my parents think?

The doorbell rings, and I can hear my parents answering it and chatting with Phoebe. They're laughing about something and the words "van" and "band" drift up. She has a whole band of villains with her? (I know I probably misheard her, but you have to admit, this sounds pretty ominous.)

I slink down the stairs and see Phoebe for the first time since she left for school a few months ago. She looks . . . different, I realize. Something's missing. The long, dangly earrings have been replaced by studs, and her hair is grown out and jammed into a ponytail. She's still wearing black leggings with a tight black tank top, and her tattoos are peeking out, but she looks like she's been in a training montage in a movie. She's always been muscular, like me, but now her muscles are sticking out in her legs. I can see hints of a six-pack, and her biceps . . . well, I can see her biceps! I'm starting to regret pretending to be sick all those days in gym class. Brains over brawn only works when you're not being sat on or put in a choke hold, and right now, Phoebe looks like she could take me.

The big difference, though, is that her face seems more like it used to when she was younger and she would come over to play with me—before she moved on to being officially A Grown-Up and got too cool/evil to bother talking to me. She still has a little makeup on, but she's lost the black lipstick and heavy eye shadow. She looks . . . well, she looks a lot more like my mom. Or me.

She spots me, and I try really hard not to freeze on the stairs.

"Hey, kid," she says, and smiles at me.

I did not work on my witty banter enough, and squeak out, "Hi!" before stumbling downstairs. I'm a little more intimidated than I expected to be: even though I know that she's not really going to be planning a bank heist (I think) over the summer, she is still older than me, and she doesn't normally talk to us much.

"Is this all your stuff?" she asks, pointing at my duffel

bag with a concerned expression. It looks like a lot to me, so I'm not sure what she's talking about, but I nod.

"Really? No second or third suitcase full of clothing?" she says, looking deadly serious.

"This is it," I say.

She glances at my parents. "We may have to go shopping at some point," she says to them, and my mom looks nervous but says that sounds good to her.

"You're sure you're okay with handling our superhero for so long?" Mom asks.

Darn it, Mom! You're going to blow my cover! I think frantically.

Phoebe just laughs. "I'm sure we'll be fine," she says, and smiles again. She doesn't look quite as tough when she grins. She grabs my duffel bag, hefting it over her shoulder like it's weightless (she really has gotten strong!), and walks it out to the porch as we all follow, and it's suddenly time for goodbye.

My parents get choked up as we try to start saying our goodbyes, and I do too, but I'm also getting excited—okay, and slightly terrified—to get this adventure started. They hug me, promising to Skype and email and bring me presents, and I promise to generally try not to make trouble for Phoebe (ha!). She's stepped back and tossed my bag into the van. Now she's playing with her phone, potentially disabling all the crazy security features she has at her apartment/lair. (That's what she'd do in a comic book anyway.)

"Ready?" she asks.

"Born ready," I say (nailed the smooth-talking retorts!), and she looks at my parents like she wants to ask them something, but I stroll casually by her and hop in the van. Mom smiles and shakes her head a little, and Phoebe does the same. Whatever she's up to, I'm ready for it.

⧚ Training Log ⧚

This may be my last entry. We're in the van and have dispensed with the small talk. She's taking me to her lair. I can barely speak or move, I'm so terrified. Sure, I know she's not actually going to boil me in a vat of acid or tie me to train tracks or anything like that. But it's been about five minutes and the silence is already freaking me out, and even scarier is the idea that we're going to have to talk to each other for the next few weeks. I'm already out of things to say, and she's not really chatty either. How are we going to survive this?

> **Superhero Tip:** Witty banter is a lot harder than it looks in comic books.

Breathing deeply,
Lindsay
(That's a mantra, not a sign-off.)

CHAPTER 5

When we pull up to her apartment building, I'm sort of disappointed that it's not a hundred stories high and made of black glass, villain-style. Instead, it's a three-story brick building only a few miles from where we live.

"It's not much," she says, "but it's home."

Her door has three different locks—at least that's kind of villainy, but most likely it's because this neighborhood borders the bad part of town—and the inside is pretty basic. At first glance anyway. I don't really know what to do with myself, so I look around. The outside might not look like much, but inside, this is a total supervillain cliché! The living room is big and light, with a plump black leather couch and a sleek metal coffee table. The living area flows into the kitchen, which has a fair amount of slightly terrifying gadgets that—if I were in a comic book—I would guess are broken-down robots, plus some seriously huge (also intimidating) knives. There are jars with blobs floating in them lining the counters. It looks like a science experiment gone horribly, horribly wrong. I make a note to stay away from there.

On the far wall, there are two crazy bikes hanging from racks. They're not like any bikes that I've ever seen before. These are painted black with bold red and gold stripes and flames, and they have crazy wheels that are entirely black, one with a clock face painted on it. One of them has bars in the front that look like the pointy tips that are meant to stab enemies, or pin them to walls. The other has tires that are three times as wide than the first's, and they're covered in knobs, like you'd need to go off-road to evade enemies. Since when does Phoebe have bikes? Clearly, there's something going on here.

I don't know what kind of crazy stuff she's gotten into, but I'm starting to get a little nervous. I touch my phone in my pocket—Mom said it's for emergencies only—and think about whether this qualifies. There's a chance I was right and she actually is up to something nefarious.

Suddenly, I hear a high-pitched shriek and jump. Did I set off an alarm? But a tiny dog pops up from behind the couch, yapping in a shrill voice, and sprints at Phoebe, springing off the ground and into her arms. Well, as springy as a dachshund can be. This one is pretty bouncy, though—maybe she's mechanically engineered it?

Normally, I know supervillains tend to have cats, but I remember that Phoebe is allergic. This tiny dog, with a drawn-out, snooty-looking nose and long black fur everywhere except its white belly, is about as close to a cat as you can get without it meowing.

"Say hello," Phoebe says, and the dachshund looks right at me and daintily raises a paw.

"Woof," it says, quietly this time.

I shake its paw, and it stares at me, like it's considering whether I'm going to be a good sidekick. It is pretty cute, even if it's potentially evil.

"This is Penguin the Pup. He's pretty cool," she says, and now I'm staring at her, not the dog. Everyone knows the Batman supervillain Penguin. That's basic Batman trivia. Is she trying to send me a message? Phoebe doesn't seem to notice, and Penguin seems pretty mild-mannered for a villainous dog. She sets down the dachshund, who stays right by her feet like a good minion, as she hefts my bag over her shoulder.

"Your room is back here," Phoebe says, walking ahead of me and carrying my bag like it doesn't weigh anything. There is a chance that she's been on some kind of super-villain muscle-growth serum that's made her this strong. I follow her down the hall, figuring I can at least make an emergency call in private if she leaves me alone in a room.

My room is at the end of the hall, and the first things I see are three tiny bikes propped against the wall. I can't believe she's even stealing bikes from kids! I'm about to say something, but she starts talking before I have the chance.

"I know it's not fancy or anything," she says, and for a second, I think she looks nervous. "It's just the spare room

I've been using for an office, so it has a futon, not a bed, but I cleared out some drawers for you."

"Looks great," I say. I actually mean it. I'm used to my babyish room at home, but this simple space with light gray walls and sun pouring in the windows—which don't have fancy, frilly curtains, just white blinds—feels super grown-up and mature. Plus, I can use her big desk for my notes and research, which is a lot cooler than the dining room table at home.

We both pause awkwardly. Well, I feel awkward anyway. I doubt Phoebe has ever been awkward in her life.

"I know you're not used to being on your own, but I know you're totally capable of taking care of yourself. You're, what, sixteen?" she says.

"I'm twelve!" I say, indignant. How did my parents let her take me for the summer?

Her lips twitch a little. Oh—she's kidding. I feel a little deflated, and a little annoyed that I let her get under my skin.

"Anyway, I spoke to your parents, and they're fine with you being in the apartment alone. But I'm not in school this summer, just working at this kind of cool place. So . . ." She drifts off, looking nervous. "If you want to maybe come to work with me tomorrow, that would be okay," she finishes in a rush, like she's as freaked out as I am by all this.

"Sure," I say coolly. Clearly, she can't be up to anything

much in this apartment; it's too small. Maybe she works at a supervillain hangout, like the Hall of Doom, or a top-secret lab. Going with her to her "work" will give me the chance to scope out her evil lair. Perfect!

"But for tonight, I figure we can just order a veggie pizza and watch a movie," she says. I think she's trying to make me feel comfortable when I should be on high alert, but after my stomach growls, I decide that pizza doesn't sound like the worst.

She leaves to make the call, but Penguin stays behind. I think he realizes that I'm feeling lonely. For an evil dachshund, he's pretty snuggly. He curls up next to me on the bed, his tiny head perched on my leg and one of his paws laid over Mr. Muffin's floppy ears. He can't be all that evil, I think as I hear Phoebe making the pizza order. Or at least he can be saved.

When the pie comes an hour later, we sit on the couch and chow down. It's great. She got a few types of cheese and a ton of vegetables I'd never think to put on a pizza—like shredded beets!—and instead of sitting in silence, we watch TV. I'm fairly certain this is her way of lulling me into a false sense of security. But to be honest, I'm so stressed out from the day that I am fully lulled by the time she gets up and says she's going to bed and that I don't have to if I'm not ready.

That snaps me awake: Would an evil person enforce a kid's bedtime or not? I decide that she must be trying to deprive me of sleep, so I fake a yawn and say I'm tired too, then stay up reading comic books with the flashlight that I brought in case of emergencies like this. I keep listening for sounds from her room, but it's quiet except for Penguin's occasional sneezing and shuffling around.

Training Log

So far, this log hasn't been discovered by Phoebe (or Penguin). I'm safe for another morning . . . and a little bored, to be honest. I'm writing this at the breakfast table, after having a normal meal—cereal—as Phoebe reads the paper in a pretty non-villainous sort of way. It's been quiet. Too quiet. I'll stay on high alert, because this is when trouble happens, at least in comic books.

> **Superhero Tip:** Never let them see you sweat. That's where meditation comes in. Clearing your mind and controlling your breath basically turn you into a superhero, since you get completely calm even in the face of a scary situation. I don't know why I didn't find out about this earlier and start doing it before science tests or gym class.

We've been acting casual, but man, she's good. I feel like I'm already giving away way too much information every time we talk. I mean, of course she knows my age, but still—why didn't I simply nod coolly when she asked if I was sixteen?

Ready for action,

Lindsay

(Getting closer.)

PENGUIN

CHAPTER 6

I get up early the next morning and settle in on the living room couch. I have no idea what to expect on my first full day in Phoebe's lair, but I'm ready for anything. When Phoebe finally comes out of her room at nine a.m., I look her up and down. She's rocking her tight black skinny jeans, leather jacket, black hat, and some weird shoes with metal points on the bottom. They must be a special kind of shoe with knives built in or something.

"I'm just going to jet over to the bank," she says.

This must be it—her first heist while I'm here! Finally, I can see where she keeps her jet packs and other supervillain gadgets. But how am I going to foil her bank robbery? If I call 911, they'll end up taking me away to stay at my aunt and uncle's.

If she's gone, I'll never get to work on my superhero training, or keep her supervillainy in check. I'm sure she'll just escape anyway. My parents will be super upset and have to leave the dig early.

Also, it's pretty unlikely she's really going to rob a bank. I mean, it's midmorning. Who robs banks this early?

"Sure, no problem," I call out, trying my best to seem indifferent.

She walks toward the wall and pulls down one of

the weird bicycles. This might be the jet that she's talking about—it looks so crazy that there must be an engine in there somewhere that gives her

a massive boost of speed for quick getaways.

"Don't go anywhere," she says with a smile. I hope she doesn't know that I'm onto her. Is she warning me to stay away so I don't try to stop her?

As soon as the door closes, I see her leap onto her bike and clip her shoes to the pedals, like she's syncing to the bike and it's part of her. In a flash, I rush to explore her room. I feel bad about it for a few seconds, but I need to search the house if I'm going to see what I'm up against. She left the door slightly open—what was she thinking?—so I don't need to try to bypass the voice identification that's obviously engaged when it closes. Too bad, really. I had a great plan for it too: a voice mail on my cell phone from Phoebe to my mom, played on speakerphone!

Flicking on the light by the door, I realize that I've struck gold. The room is filled with all sorts of crazy villain stuff. On the wall opposite the door, there's a whole workbench with really weird tools on it, like a wrench that just has a chain on the end of it. Next to the workbench, there's a stand that looks like it could either hold a person still, or maybe a robot while she works on it. Maybe it *is* a robot! There's also some stuff that's clearly for fixing her bike, like spare tires and a pump. I had no idea she was a mad-scientist-slash-engineer type of villain.

I hear the front door creak, and I bolt back to my room, then jump across the futon to grab a book, trying to look casual while my heart races. I hear footsteps down the hall, and Phoebe sticks her head in the doorway just seconds later. She doesn't seem suspicious. Phew.

"Ready to go?" she asks. For a second, I'm confused about where we're going. But then I remember that I agreed to go with her to work today. Maybe she wants me to be part of her "family business." I figure I'll just play along until I figure out exactly how to stop her.

"Sure!" I say, and bounce up.

"You might want to change into leggings or something comfortable," she suggests. "We'll roll in five minutes."

Leggings? As in, tights? The plot is thickening already—I think she's trying to get me into a super-villain costume. Instead of the leggings—clearly evil in this case—I pull on jeans and a Batman T-shirt so she knows which side of the law I'm on. But while I thought she'd be upset, she just smiles and says, "Cool shirt." She's wearing leggings and a T-shirt too, but hers says "Joyride" on it. Hmm. Is that her supervillain name?

She's changed into regular sneakers, I note. I'm still pretty confused what those first shoes were, though!

We pile into the van, and I see she has a couple more tiny bikes, probably stolen from little kids on her way to her bank heist, stacked in the back. "So where do you work?" I ask casually.

"Joyride," she says. "You're going to love it."

We're only a few minutes from her work, which looks like an aircraft hangar on the outside. It's black, though, and I can hear music pumping out of it. Seems evil enough. But when we walk in, my mouth drops open in shock.

There are kids everywhere, and all of them are on bikes like the ones Phoebe is wheeling in next to me. They're going off jumps, hopping up stairs, skidding down rails—and they look like they're having an amazing time.

"What is this place?" I ask, completely in awe. I thought we were going to a lab or something. Even if she isn't a supervillain, I figured work would be something science-y, since that's what she's in school for.

"This," Phoebe begins, gesturing energetically from wall to wall, "is Joyride. I'm a coach here."

Definitely not villainous at all, I realize as a kid with a huge smile rides by and high-fives Phoebe. I feel . . . shattered.

Training Log

What does a superhero do when it turns out that the supervillain she's spent her life planning to stop turns out to be . . . awesome?

This wasn't supposed to happen. I was supposed to spend the summer solving a mystery and saving my cousin from a life of crime before I returned home a hero. Instead, I'm just hanging out at a bike park, where I'm probably going to get made fun of, and there isn't even a corner to sit in and read. I feel tears start to well up. I know it was silly to think I'd actually get to be a hero, but deep down, I kind of believed it. Now I feel sort of dumb. I mean, look at the facts, as they're laid out:

Those little bicycles that were in my room, that I just knew she stole? Apparently, they're all BMX bikes—tiny bikes that people ride to do really cool tricks. There are teenagers and little kids zipping around on them, skidding to screeching halts to high-five, standing at the top of jumps, and generally looking cooler than I ever will.

Phoebe's clothes: sure, they're a little over the top. But as I glance around at the posters she has hanging in her office, and

check out some of the older kids in the park, she blends right in—
tons of them have piercings and tattoos, and very few aren't wearing
a lot of black.

A bank robbery? An evil lair? Seriously . . . How did I believe
that stuff?

Luckily, Phoebe takes pity on me and shows me the back room,
since I'm clearly overwhelmed. I'm hiding in her office writing this
while I sneak peeks through the window at her working at the booth.

I don't even have a cool sign-off,
Lindsay
(Well, that's not a keeper.)

CHAPTER 7

Phoebe is smiling and handing a helmet to a boy about my age with shaggy brown hair and nice eyes. He grins when she says something before he hops on his bike and pedals away. A few teenagers come in, and she does the same for them. They don't seem psyched to put

on helmets, but they do it anyway. One of them fist-bumps the young kid Phoebe just talked to. There's light streaming in from massive skylights, and announcements are blaring from the PA system, competing with loud rap music, and there are SO many people. I was ready for an epic battle, but this? I'd rather just stay in here and read.

After an hour goes by, Phoebe sticks her head in the doorway. "Linds?" she says.

I look up.

"Want to go ride?"

I shake my head. I know how to ride a bike, but going out with all those people around—watching me, laughing if I fall? I just can't do it.

She plops down in the chair on the opposite side of the desk. "You know how to ride a bike, right?"

I nod, somewhat insulted. But she's not far off. I didn't ride a lot as a kid, and I definitely don't now.

She nods and stares at me, hard. "It's pretty loud out there," she says slowly, like she's trying to figure out word by word what to say.

I nod again.

"I get it," she says, and I look at her, hard. My parents, my teachers, the therapist my parents sent me to, all of them say that. But Phoebe looks like she actually understands what I'm feeling.

"That's part of why you read those comic books so much, isn't it?" she asks. "You're not super comfortable with kids your own age?"

"More like any age," I say before I can stop myself.

"Well, do you maybe want to change that this summer?" she asks.

I freeze. Do I want to give up the dream of being a superhero and focus on just being a normal kid? My training, my grand plans of reinvention before Mom and Dad get home are over, and instead I'm here to make friends instead of fighting crime? Just like that?

Phoebe sees me pause and decides for me. "Here, put these pads on," she says. "We're going to go play."

I am not having a good summer.

⊰Training Log⊱

I only have a minute to write in here before I do something that might end in a visit to the hospital. This is not how I thought my life as a superhero was going to end. Who knows what's going to happen out there. . . . I haven't been on a bike since I was a little kid pedaling in the driveway, and Phoebe wants me to ride on wooden ramps? At least I have my journal here with me so I can make what might be my final entry.

If this is the end, thank you for reading. I hope someone will one day find this and share my story.

Eternally yours,
Lindsay
(That might have to be it.)

CHAPTER 8

I'm wearing kneepads and elbow pads. I have a giant helmet strapped to my head. I'm holding a bike at the top of a massive drop into a pit. And yes, the pit is filled with foam, but this still may be the scariest moment of my life. That foam looks pretty solid. I'm not actually sure I can make my legs stop shaking. Phoebe is standing behind me, looking ahead too. I can picture how this panel would look in a comic book: her face cool and confident, with just a hint of a smile starting. Mine . . . well, I'm sure it looks like I'm about to plunge to my death.

"I'm about to plunge to my death," I say.

"You're going to be fine," she says. "Think of it as practice for flying, superhero-style. You think Supergirl was perfect at takeoff when she first got her powers?"

She clearly knows how to get me. We've already covered the

really easy stuff: pedaling, cruising around, and—most importantly—stopping. Which, by the way, I did not realize meant grabbing a brake lever with my hand. My bike at home has a coaster brake, so you have to pedal backward to stop. I think. I'm not entirely positive of that, since it's been a hangout for spiders in the corner of the garage for years.

Riding bikes never seemed very cool before, but being here, I'm seeing it differently now. I remember hearing girls at school laughing at one girl, Danielle, who rode her bike to school all of last year. Thinking about it now, I make a silent vow to be nicer to her and try to make friends next year, especially since I may start riding my bike to school too. Maybe we can even ride together! (If my mom lets me, that is.)

I'm getting ahead of myself, considering I haven't actually started pedaling down the ramp yet, and the thought is terrifying.

Phoebe yanks me out of my elaborate daydream as she cues something up on her phone and hits play. I immediately recognize the strains of music, but I'm shocked she knew just what to put on. It's the theme music that introduces Superman in the cartoons I watch every weekend.

And all at once, my legs stop shaking. I stand up straight, put one foot on the pedal, look forward, and kick off with my other foot.

The bike and I roll down the few feet of wooden ramp and then off a tiny cliff with a slight tilt to it. It's like running and diving off a diving board, but on a bike and over a pit of foam. A few hours ago, I would have assumed that Phoebe was trying to torture me, that this was her diabolical death machine. But the way she's smiling and encouraging me, I know this might be the best thing I've ever done.

I get in two pedal strokes before I'm off the ramp, and then it happens. I'm flying, actually flying, still holding on to the bike. This is how Supergirl feels, how Wonder Woman flies. It's only half of a second in the air, but it feels like forever, and when I hit the foam blocks that fill the giant pit, I can't stop smiling—and it doesn't hurt at all. Phoebe sticks her hand over the side and I grab it. She isn't a supervillain at all. She's my cousin, and she gets me.

"Can we do it again?" I ask before I'm even out, scrambling to pull my bike with me.

"Let's get back to the basics first," she says. "I don't normally start anyone on the foam pit—but that was really good. You might be a natural at this!" We high-five, and I only kind of miss her hand. My glasses got a bit knocked around by the foam, so my vision isn't the best.

And I've never felt better about myself in my life.

≋ Training Log ≋

Riding a bike for the first time in years, learning that my cousin isn't evil, and the extreme volume of music, voices, and tires squealing in that park has been a lot to take in, but I'm not just tired—I'm trying to figure out what's next for the summer. My plan to complete this manual as a hero-in-training has flown out the window. Part of me wants to throw this journal in the dumpster and give up on the whole training thing, but there's this glimmer in the back of my mind that maybe—just maybe—there's a different kind of training I could be doing instead.

What if I want to be a super bike rider instead? It does seem like superheroes and cyclists dress pretty similar: a lot of spandex, a lot of bright colors and logos on their chests, so basically, they're kind of the same thing. And hey, this is my journal, right? So in here, I can be as super as I want to be.

Maybe Phoebe was meant to be my mentor, not my archnemesis, all along. Kind of like Batman and Robin, but I can dress a lot better than the Boy Wonder ever did.

Superhero Tip: There's more than one way to fly.

Kind of, sort of becoming a superhero,
Lindsay
(Umm . . . maybe not.)

CHAPTER 9

Because I'm thinking so hard, I'm quiet in the car on the way home from Joyride. It's been the best day, and Phoebe has been awesome. She's quiet too, and I start to feel a little bad that I'm not talking to her after all she did for me today.

"That was really fun," I say.

"It's pretty great, isn't it?" she says.

"I felt like a superhero," I say, and wait for her to laugh at me.

"I know exactly what you mean," she says, looking serious. "I started riding there a couple of years ago when I was feeling pretty down on myself. My dad suggested I check it out after he read about it. I didn't expect to like it, but I ended up loving it so much that I've started coaching and working there. I was a lot like you—I wasn't into sports, and I just wanted to stay home and read. And that's cool too," she says quickly, seeing my face fall. "But don't you ever want to be out doing the things that the people in those comics are doing?"

She's exactly right. That's what I've been missing—the real-world training. And yeah, after today, I'm starting to see that I might not have an archnemesis after all, but that doesn't totally mean I can't be super, does it?

The more I think about it, the more it makes sense: Superman didn't meet Lex Luthor right when he discovered his powers. It took a while. Maybe my chance to be a hero will come with time, as I develop my powers.

"Can I come back and keep riding?" I ask hopefully.

"You can if you want me to coach you," she says. "And I have a bit of a secret I've been keeping from you too."

Just when I think I finally know what she's up to . . .

"I have a bike for you—it's just my old one, but it's a pretty good one that I think you'll like," she says. "And part of why your parents wanted you to stay with me was because they were hoping I'd be able to get you to come to Joyride and start riding."

"Seriously?" I snort a little bit and then start giggling, and Phoebe starts laughing too. I thought they were ditching me with my archnemesis, who I'm starting to realize isn't exactly evil—more misunderstood. (Just like Batman.) Instead, my parents are trying to get me to . . . ride bikes? The idea seems so bizarre that I can't really make sense of it.

I imagine them scheming with Phoebe to make me athletic, and it's somehow hilarious.

"Why are we laughing?" she asks, not stopping.

"I . . . I thought you were a supervillain!" I say, bursting into giggles again. But Phoebe doesn't keep laughing.

I mean, I did think she was evil, but she also just taught me to do the coolest thing I've ever done. I'm not sure she's ready to hear I thought she was my nemesis . . . but she deserves the truth.

"Well, you know, with the hair and the makeup and the clothes and the tattoos and the weird bikes and shoes and the van and everything," I say, all in a rush. And as I'm saying it, I realize how it sounds, and that she might really be mad at me, that I might have ruined everything.

"Oh, man." She sighs and looks straight ahead through the windshield. "Lindsay," she starts, and before she keeps going, I cut her off.

"But now I know you're not, and I'm really, really sorry!"

"You do know that supervillains like the ones in comic books aren't real, right? There are bad people in the world, but most of us—just because we have tattoos and wear a lot of makeup—are generally not evil," she says, and seems pretty grumpy. But then her face shifts a little, and she just looks sad. "I know sometimes I might look different, but I don't want you to think that I'm a bad person because of it. I don't have some kind of criminal plan for world domination or anything, okay?"

"I know you're not evil," I say. "And I knew that before today. It's just . . . well, how can I be a superhero if I don't have a supervillain to fight?"

"You know, in a weird way, I get that," she says. "But maybe we can work on making you more super on the bike instead."

I nod excitedly. "That's what I was thinking!"

She continues. "And by the way, the van isn't for my band of villain friends. It's for my actual band. It's just me and a couple of girlfriends: Phoebe and the Chainbreakers."

She makes a lot of sense. But still . . . "Just one more thing," I say before I can stop myself.

"Sure," she says.

"You really didn't rob a bank this morning?"

"I rode to the bank on my bike," she says, confused.

"But what about those shoes with the hidden metal?" I ask, because that still doesn't make sense.

"You'll have a pair soon enough, if you're training to ride bikes," she says. "Those are cycling shoes! They clip onto pedals for certain types of bikes. Not the ones we're starting with, but eventually we'll get you on different types of bikes."

"Oh," I say, feeling a little ridiculous. "But come on, those shoes do look really goofy."

Phoebe just shakes her head and laughs.

⇒ Training Log ⇐

Dinner is over, and I'm pondering what my next move will be. Really, what my mind keeps coming back to is the bike park and how awesome it felt to take that jump. Scary, but awesome. Maybe jumping can be my "thing." Every superhero has a few key moves: Superman has the lasers he shoots out of his eyes, for example, and while I obviously can't do that, maybe sweet jumps can be my equivalent. I noticed some kids in the park were jumping pretty high without even having a cushy foam pit to land in, so maybe by the end of the summer, if I really work at it, I can get to that point. But maybe I won't ask Phoebe about jumping just yet—she might not be evil, but I do get the feeling she's going to push me pretty hard on the bike as it is, and I don't want to give her any crazy ideas!

> **Superhero Tip:** Have a signature move.

Called away by ice cream,
Lindsay
(Factually accurate, but, sadly, not always.)

CHAPTER 10

"So what would your costume be?" Phoebe asks, totally seriously, as she scoops more ice cream into her mouth. We had fajitas that Phoebe made from our grandma's recipe (I'd never admit it to anyone in my family, but Phoebe's homemade salsa is the best that I've ever had), but Phoebe says there's always room for ice cream.

"Well, not like that," I say, pointing at the TV screen, where Wonder Woman is battling an alien while wearing what is basically a bathing suit. (Phoebe said that since she picked what we did during the day, it was my turn to pick the movie. And it turns out she actually has a few of the same movies as me, so I didn't need to dig through my bag to find my favorite Wonder Woman cartoon. She already had it—the special-edition one with all the bonus features!)

"Yeah, that might stand out if you wore that around town. Plus, you'd be super cold. And your mom might kill you." She giggled. "But really, did you ever draw a costume for yourself?"

I have been working on my costume in my Wonder Woman notebook, though I wouldn't admit it to just anyone. "Yes! Let me go get it," I say, surprising myself and scrambling up to grab my bag. I guess Phoebe isn't just anyone anymore.

As I'm running back to the room with my notebook in hand, Penguin hops up on the counter and starts begging for fajita leftovers, paws waving in the air.

"Phoebe, how come you named him Penguin anyway?"

"You're not the only one who loves Batman," she says, and I turn around, startled. "I thought he looked like a tiny penguin when I got him, and it seemed really appropriate, since I'm into comic books."

"Really?"

"Really," she says, and I feel a lot better about telling her everything. I should have known that she was a kindred spirit, even when I still thought she was evil: superheroes and supervillains actually have more in common than you'd think, if you read between the lines. We all care deeply about saving or destroying the world, but either way, we're extremely passionate about it.

"I didn't think he was totally evil," I say, and reach over to pet him.

"Now, let's see these costume sketches. I bet they're pretty awesome—and I know they're going to be smart, right?" She arches her eyebrow at me and points at the screen, where one of the villains has ripped Wonder Woman's skirt, making it even shorter than before. "I definitely don't think your mom would approve of that."

I sit down, open to the page, and show her. "I was watching a bunch of ballet movies with a girl from school a year ago, and seeing ballet costumes and workout gear gave me a great idea for a superhero costume that's practical but still totally wearable to school. That is, if Mom would ever let me wear it." The picture is a girl wearing leggings with a sleeveless leotard over them, a short shrug sweater, a midthigh-length skirt, and a pair of high-top sneakers. Her hair is tied back in a ponytail with a scarf wrapped around it.

"See?" I say, pointing to parts of the costume. "When I'm walking around school, I just look like I'm wearing a cute skirt and sweater. But then crime happens, and bam! Skirt and sweater are both easy to take off, leaving me in a leotard and tights, and sensible shoes. Plus, the scarf can be used as a weapon, lasso, or rope."

Phoebe looks like she's about to laugh, and I can feel disappointment welling up in my chest. She doesn't get it. But to my surprise, she starts to look thoughtful.

"I think it would be even more incognito—that means sort of undercover—if you switched it up," she says. "So you could change it and make different outfits in the same style, like sometimes use a funky leathery material for your tights, or maybe a metallic leotard," she adds, getting even more excited. "And you could switch the fabric and color of the skirt and sweater so it's more stylish. Come on." She grabs my hand, pulls me into her room, and starts flinging things out of drawers.

How many non-supervillains have not one, but four pairs of metallic tights in different colors? And how many have multiple leotards?

I know we're becoming friends, but I still find it really hard to believe she's never been tempted by the dark side.

"A lot of the kids at Joyride just wear leggings and whatever shirt they want when they're riding," she says. "So I don't see why you shouldn't do that this summer. I have some stuff from a couple of years ago that might fit you."

Before I know it, I'm in front of her mirror wearing black leggings with a long emerald-green tank top, a short fake-leather vest, and my black high-top sneakers. (I wanted the metallic tights, but Phoebe says metallic and leather definitely don't mix.) My hair is in a crazy braid that Phoebe says is a "fishtail," and she tosses me a long pendant necklace with a silver chain, and a big purple amethyst armband with rocky, raw silver edges.

"You can wear this to dress it up a little, but not while you're riding," she says. "It kind of goes from sporty to mystical, right?"

I look in the mirror, and I actually look kind of . . . cool. Having a little bit more muscle than most girls my age seems pretty sweet, especially with a silver armband pulled up around my bicep—kind of like Wonder Woman's amulets—and an outfit that isn't baggy everywhere.

"You know, I think I like it," I say, and Phoebe grins.
She comes and stands next to me, and we look in the
mirror together.

"You look like you could kick some serious butt," she
says. I feel like I really could. And I'm pretty stoked that
I no longer have to figure out how to kick my cousin's.

Training Log

It's been a long day, but I can't stop thinking about how much fun it was talking about clothes and trying some on, and having someone actually take my ideas seriously. Mom never really got what I was doing, and I never had a close girl friend to talk to, so it's kind of new and exciting to chat with Phoebe about it. Even though I said I was going to bed, I'm not tired at all, just writing with my flashlight and sketching more designs. Okay, fine. I'm a little tired, and blinking a lot, but maybe I can get through one more design. . . .

> **Superhero Tip:** Sequins, while a nice shiny touch, are impractical whether superhero-ing or bike riding. And not very easy to wash, apparently.

Zzzzzzz,
Lindsay
(No, I didn't write that in my sleep, but wouldn't it be cool if I had?)

CHAPTER 11

"Time to get up!" Phoebe shouts, sticking her head in the door to my room. I'm still snuggled under my Batman comforter with my not-so-super-but-still-cozy stuffed bunny, and I shove Mr. Muffin under the covers so Phoebe doesn't see. "Time for breakfast! We have to head out to Joyride in an hour," she says, and before she closes the door again, she adds, "And you know, Mr. Muffin used to be mine."

Man, I can't get anything past her. But I shouldn't be surprised, since she's the one who brought me the Batman comforter last night, like she knew I'd need it. That also used to be hers, apparently. I throw on my clothes and head to the kitchen.

"Okay, one more villain question: what's with those weird jars on the counter?" I can't help but ask. I know now that there's probably a rational explanation, but still . . . they do look pretty gross. There are blobs floating in the brownish water, in giant containers. It reminds me of last year's science fair when an experiment this kid did on mold went a little overboard.

"That's kombucha," Phoebe explains. "It's a fermented tea that's really good for your stomach. It's really expensive and you can usually only get it in health food stores, so I started brewing it myself because I like the taste and it keeps my guts happy."

Well. That makes sense, even if it is kind of a letdown.

"You can try some," she says, going over to the fridge and grabbing a small bottle off the shelf. Tentatively, I take a sip . . . and it's delicious! Acidic but a little sweet, and really refreshing.

"This is good," I admit sheepishly.

"Thanks," she says, sitting back down next to me after grabbing a bottle for herself.

Phoebe tells me the plan for the day over scrambled eggs with spinach, which she swears is superhero food, but which I think may be at least slightly sinister. "I run a class called Shred Girls, and I have two of them coming in today for the first session," she says. "I think you should do the class. Ali and Jen are pretty cool. You'll like them."

My stomach drops. "I sort of thought it was going to be just us," I say slowly, trying to think of a reason to stay home. And I wouldn't be lying if I said my stomach hurt—it's starting to ache thinking about meeting and talking to new people.

"I know how hard it is making friends, especially at your age," Phoebe says. "But just try today, and if you really hate it, I won't make you go again—and after the session, we can spend my lunch break playing on the mini jump line. Just us."

Part of me wants to just refuse to go, but the other part of me is aching to feel that flying feeling again.

"Oh, and one more thing to convince you?" Phoebe says, grinning. "I haven't shown you your new bike."

She walks back to her room, and a second later, she's wheeling out the coolest bike that I've ever seen—it must have been hidden in her closet since I got here. It's the same emerald green as the tank top she gave me last night, with purple grips on the ends of the handlebars, a purple saddle, and purple spokes on the wheels. It matches my outfit perfectly.

"I know superheroes stick to a color scheme, and I thought this would be perfect for you," she says casually.

I look at her accusingly. "You're trying to bribe me!"

"Yep," she says unapologetically. "Did it work?"

"I'll be in the car," I say, as dignified as I possibly can be when I'm practically hugging the bike. It has a purple chain—I didn't think they made bike chains in any color other than silver!—and glitter in the paint. It's the perfect bike. And it's mine. But as I wheel it out the door and bring it over to the van, I look at my cousin. She's walking behind me, wearing black leggings with a loose gray three-quarter-sleeve top that hangs off one shoulder, a silver sports bra peeking out to match her silver Vans slip-on shoes. Her hair is braided to the side, and her silver hoop earrings go halfway up her ear, and tattoos on her shoulder peek out of her top. Her bike—the same size as mine—is black, with silver accents to match. She looks like the coolest person in the world, not the scariest. I put down my bike (my bike!), and before I can think about what I'm doing, I'm running at her and tackling her in a flying hug.

"Thanks," I mutter as she hugs me back, stumbling a little but managing to stabilize us before we fall into the bushes.

"Let's roll," she says, shifting the hug into a bit of a headlock on me, but it seems more cousiny than villain-ous, so I roll with it happily. She's got a huge grin on her face as she hops into the driver's seat, so I know that the hug was just right.

When we get to Joyride, it's still loud and scary walking in, but this time, I'm feeling a lot cooler with my amazing bike. Phoebe walks in front of me and leads the way over to the spot where classes meet, and I start to feel way more nervous.

"What if they don't like me?" I whisper.

"I know it sounds like something your parents say, but I promise, people aren't as scary as you think. I bet these girls are going to be just as nervous as you are about you not liking them," Phoebe responds, which makes me feel a little bit better. Not fully better, and I don't completely believe her, but I'm trying to remember my own rule about never letting people see you sweat. Probably good advice regardless of supervillainy.

As we wait for a couple of minutes, I scan the entrance looking for potential Alis and Jens. So far, I've only seen boys, and a couple of really young girls that Phoebe says are too young to be in our class. But then a girl about my age walks in. And she looks so cool that I'm instantly terrified.

"Ali, over here!" Phoebe calls.

Ali glides over on her bike, looking totally at home in Joyride. She's wearing a button-down flannel and knee-length baggy shorts, and her backpack has a flat-brim baseball cap hanging off it. Her red hair spikes out when she takes her helmet off, and she looks so cool and comfortable that I start adjusting my glasses and fiddling with my braid, trying to make myself invisible behind Phoebe. Her bike doesn't quite match her outfit—it's bright blue with white accents—but it looks just right for her.

"Hey, Phoebe!" Ali says, smiling.

"Ali, meet my cousin Lindsay. She's staying with me for the summer," Phoebe says, and pushes me forward. Ali smiles and sticks up her hand for a high five.

I high-five her, and she looks over and rolls her eyes a little as another girl our age walks in the door. Phoebe waves the other girl over. This girl has to be Jen, and she walks toward us with her helmet in her hand, pushing her all-silver bike next to her, not looking overly happy.

"Hi, Jen," Phoebe says cheerfully. Jen reminds me immediately of the girls who are kind of mean to me at school—the ones who don't tease me to my face but who I sometimes hear talking about me at lunch or in class. She's got blond hair with purple streaks (wow!), and she's wearing jean shorts and a really cool black tank top with silver streaks. As she walks up to us, Phoebe makes the introductions.

"Jen, meet Lindsay and Ali. Ali is here visiting her mom for the summer, and she's been messing around on the BMX bike for a couple of years now, though she mountain bikes more often than she BMXs. Lindsay is my cousin and she's in town to train with me for the summer." I look at her, grateful for making me sound like a pro, not just some kid who's never been on a BMX bike. "And, Ali and Lindsay, Jen here is one of the fastest twelve-year-old road cyclists in the country."

"Umm, Phoebe?" I ask. "What's the difference between the BMX, mountain, and road?"

"Right, sorry!" she replies. "So BMX bikes are these small ones you've been riding, and they're mostly for in the park and doing tricks."

I nod.

"Road bikes are those bikes with the super-skinny tires, and the people who ride them are usually wearing spandex, like superheroes," she continues. "And mountain bikes are the ones with wider handlebars and wide, knobby tires for riding on trails—the people who ride them are usually in baggier shorts and T-shirts."

"Thanks," I say gratefully. I can picture Jen flying by on the road in (probably pink) spandex, and Ali speeding over stones and roots rocking the same outfit she's wearing now.

"Hey, guys," Jen says. When Phoebe walks off to sign us all in, Jen leans in to us. "Are you really stoked about this?"

"Absolutely," Ali says, a little too loudly. "I'm hoping to win this summer's jumping tournament here."

"For sure," I manage to squeak out.

Jen looks kind of disappointed. "I'm only here because my parents said I had to," says Jen, then adds, almost proudly, "They said I needed to learn to relax, because I was getting too focused on winning. So they told me I couldn't ride a bike for a while, unless it was for fun—can you believe that?"

"Then how did you end up here?" Ali asks.

"I got them to let me come here because they think I'll get 'socialized,' instead of spending all my time at my grandparents' house for this month," Jen says, emphasizing "socialized" with air quotes. "It's not the riding I want to be doing, but at least I'm still riding." She seems more proud of her cycling ban than upset about it, so Ali and I just nod sympathetically. Clearly, neither of us gets her deal—I want to ask more, and I can tell Ali's trying to think of a good way to ask a question, but we're at a loss for words.

Thankfully, Phoebe walks back. "You girls ready to play?" she asks, and we all nod.

We start with some really basic stuff that Phoebe taught me yesterday—the rules of Joyride, how to follow the arrows around and ride on the right side of the trails that lead all over the building, where the bathrooms are, and how to stop our bikes. Ali already knows all of it and keeps talking over Phoebe a little. Phoebe doesn't seem to mind, and Ali's chatter lets me keep quiet and stay behind both her and Jen.

We're not doing anything like the jump that I did yesterday, but in some ways, it's just as scary since I'm trying hard to stay behind Jen without running into her, especially since we keep speeding up and slowing down as we navigate around the park. Bike riding . . . not as easy as I remembered! There's a lot more precision involved than I thought—which I realize as I try to slow down but instead manage to drive my front tire into a low wall. Smooth, Linds. Real smooth.

But it's exhilarating at the same time: trying to stay right behind Jen almost feels like I'm in a video game, but my bike is the controller. After the first few laps around the park just to get used to our bikes, I start sort of figuring it out, which means that it's time for Phoebe to tell us to stop and take a quick break.

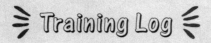

Training Log

Okay, time for some training rules for this new plan of mine: to be a superhero on the bike by the end of summer.

Superhero Tip: First rule: Love your bike like it's your favorite stuffed animal or your pet. That means taking care of it. When Phoebe walked out of the room, she stopped, turned, and told me if she ever saw it with a dent, scuff, or scratch that was caused from me leaving it lying around, and not from getting "too rad" (her words, not mine), she'd take it back. And that I'd better keep it clean. Now I understand why her van is so meticulously tidy. She's not a supervillain; she's just really, really careful with her stuff. Which, I suppose, is good advice for anyone.

Anyway, I know that the Justice League is a cool group to be part of. But I'm more a loner like Batman (though he does have Robin and Batgirl, I guess). Joining clubs has never been my thing, and having to embarrass myself in front of girls I don't know at all? Nightmare.

At least I have a cool bike. It's sort of like bringing the Bat-mobile to a Justice League meeting.

But it turns out that Phoebe's training program is more than just riding bikes or owning a nice one. Before we get to hit any of the cool jumps that line the back half of the park, she has us off the bikes and on the floor doing what she calls planks. I've seen videos of people planking—doing planks in weird spots—but have you ever tried it? It's hard!

Regretfully yours,
Lindsay
(That's too whiny.)

CHAPTER 12

My arms are shaking with the effort of holding a high push-up position, and Phoebe's suggestion that I put my butt down and look forward is more distracting than helpful. I almost fall over a couple of times, and when I sneak a glance at Jen and Ali, they both seem to be doing a lot better than me. But I don't want to be the first one to topple, so I stay up, arms shaking.

Phoebe explained that core stability is going to help us with our riding—so our stomach muscles need to be in good shape. And apparently, planks are a good way to get there. So I stay up.

That is, until I just can't anymore, and slowly lower my knees to the ground. I can feel my face get red with embarrassment. I'm sure that the other girls are going to make fun of me. But when I look over, they haven't even noticed that I'm down—they're turning red too, trying to stay up. Ali finally stands up, wiping her hands on her shorts and breathing hard, and only when she's up does Jen collapse in a heap, panting.

"Why would you do this to us?" Jen whines.

I'm thinking the same thing, and I wonder if Phoebe really does have a diabolical plan of some kind. After all, why else would she be torturing us?

"Guys, if you want to ride bikes well, you need to have a strong foundation," she says. "It's not all cool tricks and crazy stunts. There's a lot of base work that goes into building up to be a great cyclist. Now, get on your bikes and do three laps of the outside of the park."

We all groan but grab our bikes. "I thought this was going to be all jumping," Jen says, but she seems happy to be doing more actual riding. She rips around a corner without touching her brakes, while I slowly pedal through it, holding mine so tightly that I basically am stopped right in the middle of the turn.

Phoebe waves me over before I hit the next turn. "Try to slow down before you go into a corner; it'll feel a lot better," she tells me. I nod, but that seems ridiculous. Why would I slow down even earlier?

As the next corner comes up, Phoebe yells, "Brake now!" as I'm still thirty feet away. I slow down a little, listening to her. As the corner comes up, she shouts, "Let go of your brakes," and I do. The corner comes, and I smoothly (okay, not smoothly but a little more steadily) get around it.

Half a lap in, I can feel myself sweating. Ali and Jen are just about to turn a corner, but I'm falling so far behind that, as soon as they make the turn, I'll lose sight of them. Maybe I'm not cut out for this. I think of my backpack in the corner, full of comic books, with a longing that I didn't know I could feel. Sitting down to read has never sounded so good. And reading always sounds good to me!

As I'm about to flip my bike and race back to my back-pack, Phoebe glides up next to me. Man, she's sneaky!

"You know," she says, lowering her voice, "those two have been riding for years already. You're on your second day of riding."

"So?" I can't help but ask moodily, scowling at the air ahead of me where Ali and Jen used to be.

"So they have a lot more practice and they're going to be faster at first," she says. "With a little work, you'll be right behind them."

"But still behind?" I grump.

"For now," she tells me, and pats me on the shoulder before pulling over to the side and whipping out her phone. "Smile!" she says, and snaps a picture while I'm caught between a snarl and a grin.

Now, that's a Christmas card.

But I do keep riding. And as the first lap of the room finishes, my legs aren't burning as much, and my breathing has settled down. I'm not going any faster—but I'm not getting any slower either.

Things are starting to feel less terrifying and more natural the more I'm riding, and as I turn one corner, suddenly I can see Ali and Jen again. I'm sweating and breathing hard, and when I try to go a little faster to catch up to them, I swerve just a bit and smash my shoulder against the wall. It explodes with pain, and I grunt as I topple off my bike.

For a second, I'm afraid I'm going to start crying, huddling in a ball on the floor—it hurts and I hate this stupid sport. Wonder Woman never gets hurt like this. . . . I mean, sure, she has to battle pretty big monsters and I'm guessing she's crashed her invisible jet, but she has super strength and I clearly don't. To add insult to injury, I'm also tangled in and under my bike, and can't quite figure out how to get up. After a few seconds, the pain in my shoulder eases—okay, maybe it wasn't as bad as I thought—and my face is red more with embarrassment than actual hurt. Klutzes probably shouldn't ride bikes, I think. Maybe I should return it to Phoebe . . . that is, if I can ever get back on my feet.

"Need a hand?"

I crane my neck (oww!) and there's a boy my age, reaching down toward me, and of course, I realize, it's the cute one I spotted yesterday. I can feel my face turn bright red. Great. The dream boy talks to me but only because I just embarrassed myself in front of him. Now I've completely forgotten about my shoulder and am focused entirely on looking as casual as one can when one is trapped under one's bike. That is to say, not very.

"Don't worry about it," he says, like he's reading my mind. "I've already crashed three times today. It means you're trying, right?"

He pulls me to standing, and I just nod dumbly, my brain racing to think of something remotely witty to say

in response. "I'm Dave," he says, smiling. He has shaggy light brown hair, and he's wearing flannel, jeans, and a lot more safety gear than most of the other kids. Maybe he really has already crashed a few times today. His hand is calloused, and I can see scars on it as he steadies me. "You okay? Did you hit your head?" He looks really concerned.

"No . . . I'm just awkward," I blurt out, and instantly wish I could take it back.

"Okay, Awkward," he says. "But is there another name I could call you?" He doesn't look like he's laughing at me, but he is smiling.

"Lindsay," I say, impressed that I managed to answer a question correctly.

"Well, have a good ride, Lindsay. Don't worry about that fall. It really does happen all the time," he says, getting back on his bike. "Maybe I'll see you around again. I really like your bike."

I stand there for a minute, slightly stupefied, but internally I'm jumping up and down.

Maybe this sport isn't so bad after all.

Either way, I really owe Phoebe for giving me this bike.

Training Log

Cute boy and embarrassing moment, scary girls but no embarrassing moments—I think I would call this day an overall win. But it turns out actual, real-life training that's not in my head or in the basement makes a girl really, really hungry. Thankfully, Phoebe says we can get a snack on the way home. Otherwise, I was going to consider eating this journal.

> **Superhero Tip:** Always have snacks on hand. (I'll remember that for next time.)

Famished,

Lindsay

(Accurate, but hopefully not all the time.)

Dave

CHAPTER 13

We drive immediately to the diner, thankfully, and after Phoebe orders, we sit down to wait for our disco fries, my favorite "not allowed at home because it's crazy unhealthy" snack: fries with cheese curds and gravy on top.

"So be honest," she says, sipping her black coffee while I chug water like it's going out of style. Riding bikes makes you thirsty! "How did you like today's practice?"

"It was good," I say slowly. "But I don't think the girls like me very much."

"Did you try talking to them?" she asks.

"No," I admit. "I thought they were going to laugh when I couldn't hold a plank as long as they could or do the same tricks." The waitress sets down our fries.

"Here's the thing," Phoebe says, snagging a fry and waving it for emphasis as steam comes off it. "Did you notice the time Ali almost fell off the bike in that easy corner? Or when Jen tripped walking back to her bike?"

I definitely didn't and shake my head. (My mouth is full of delicious fries. They are maybe too hot to cram into my mouth but worth it.)

"Exactly," she says. "You didn't notice that, and they certainly didn't notice you not holding a plank as long as they did. Besides, they know you're new at this. But I know that the worst part for you isn't the riding. Admit it: it's the chatting."

"Talking to people is really hard," I say, and I know that sounds like a joke, but I really do mean it.

"I get it, because I'm the same way," Phoebe says. "To be honest, I was even a little scared of Ali and Jen when I met them. But if you don't talk to the other girls, you can't expect them to talk to you. It's a bummer, but people like us can look like we're stuck-up when we're really just scared."

If I hadn't swallowed, the fries would be falling out of my mouth, which is currently hanging open. She's right, I realize. I didn't notice what they were doing or how they were riding, really, because I was so worried about me.

"I still don't think Jen wants to talk to me," I say stubbornly. Because, to be honest, she didn't seem that friendly.

"Think about it," Phoebe says, waving a fry at me. "Did you really want to talk to her? She doesn't seem like the kind of girl you'd usually hang out with, so maybe she felt the same about you. But you two are here for the whole summer, and you do both have bikes in common, so maybe you do have something to talk about."

I hate when she makes points like that. "I guess," I mutter.

And okay, I admit, using Phoebe's logic, she does have a point. Since I haven't been starting conversations with

Ali or Jen, I might actually be the snobby one here. Especially since I already know Phoebe and they're the new kids in the area. And thinking about that, it reminds me of being in school and not having any friends. Maybe it's not that kids aren't talking to me.

Maybe it's that I'm not talking to them.

I might have to rethink a lot of things. But before I spend too much time quietly thinking, I should probably take the first step toward actually making two friends, since I have a captive audience with them at Joyride.

"Can I borrow your phone?" I ask Phoebe. She hands it over. I know she has Jen's and Ali's numbers in there from today, so I try not to let my hands shake too much as I call Ali. She seemed more outgoing and inclined to be friendly, and I think she'll be easier to start with. Jen, I might need to work up to a little more, but I'll get there.

"Hello . . . hello?" Oh no. Ali actually answers.

I freeze a bit but force myself to act calm. "Hey, Ali, it's Lindsay, Phoebe's cousin from today."

"What's up?" She sounds friendly enough, and she didn't hang up—that's a good sign.

"Just wondering if you were going to Joyride later this week."

"Absolutely. I'll be there at four tomorrow afternoon so I can work on that jump line again. What about you?"

"Four?" I look over at Phoebe, raising my eyebrows, and she nods.

"We'll be there. Want to ride together?" I ask boldly. Well, it probably comes out as more of a squeak. But in my head, it's pretty bold. It would be written in bold in a comic book font, at least.

"Sure, see you then!"

I say goodbye and hang up, breathing a little fast. Phoebe puts her closed hand out for a fist bump. I don't know that I handle the bump with the proper etiquette, but we make some kind of hand-to-hand contact, so I'll call it a win.

"That wasn't so hard, was it?" she asks smugly, and I can't find a single reason to disagree. It turns out talking to kids isn't really that scary, once you get started. I'm actually excited to get to the park tomorrow to hang out, even if there's a nagging voice in the back of my head already wondering what the heck we'll talk about.

Training Log

I still don't know how my cousin turned into someone who coaches people to ride bikes, but it's starting to seem like a really cool career path. Of course, I think I need a whole bunch more practice, but I have a pretty great starting point. And today, I sort of started coming up with a comic-book-worthy idea of where I want to be by the end of the summer. While I was in the bathroom at Joyride, I noticed a flyer tacked on the stall door. It was for a BMX jumping competition that's coming up in a few weeks, and it said there were three levels—beginner, intermediate, and advanced. I'm a beginner, right? And I don't think I'm the only one who noticed: I'm pretty sure it's the contest that Ali was talking about it when she first came in. The prizes? An amazing-looking gold bike frame—and there's one for each of the three categories. (I love mine, but still . . . gold!) You also get a check that's supposed to go toward your training for the year—lessons, a pass to Joyride, coaching, that kind of stuff. I've never played a sport in my life or competed in something that

 wasn't for school, but I tore the flyer down and stuffed it in my pocket. I don't know if I want to talk to Phoebe about doing the competition yet, but after looking at the jumps today, I absolutely,

positively know that I want to be able to do the cool tricks some of the other kids were doing. I could imagine myself in their shoes, I could feel my heart beating faster, and I loved it.

Superhero Tip: Any good superhero story has a climactic moment of high drama. Pick one for yourself . . . like a competition.

Getting a little closer to a superhero plot,
Lindsay
(Hopefully, this is correct, but it's not really a sign-off.)

CHAPTER 14

I accidentally managed to find the best teacher around when it comes to jumping, apparently. As we finished up at the park today, Phoebe grabbed one of the bikes and hit one of the bigger jumps, spinning her handlebars while she soared through the air before landing and hopping off. She had a huge smile on her face, and the kid she was talking to before she dropped into the jump line—that's the technical lingo—was staring, gobsmacked.

The jump lines at Joyride consist of five wooden bumps (or jumps, I suppose) that you drop in to. That means you start on a little platform and roll down a ramp before going up the first of the bumps, and as you go over each, you jump so you don't really touch the top. You sort of float on the small ones, and as the bumps get bigger, the hops you do over each get bigger as well, so you're flying over the top before touching down on the backside. It's pretty cool.

Phoebe has kind of gone from supervillain to superhero in my book. I think I get why my parents wanted me to spend time with her.

I hate when they're right—it's so annoying. And it happens so often! On my last call with them—a shaky Skype connection, but at least I could see their faces—

they seemed completely surprised that Phoebe had actually gotten me onto a bike and that I was excited about it. I even showed them the bike Phoebe gave me, and told them about the jumps that I was working on. They were a little stunned, honestly. . . . But even more stunned when I told them it was okay if they didn't bring me back any artifacts. I don't need some old Estonian vase imbued with superpowers anymore; I'm figuring my own out.

From my backpack, I pull out my notebook and look down at the sketches Phoebe helped me draw last night of my costume. And then I look over at my reflection in the window—jeans, baggy T-shirt—and back down to the sketch. I think about how cool Jen looked with purple streaks in her hair and how comfortable Ali seemed in her shorts. I don't want to look like either of them, but they both seem so much older than me, so much . . . more than me. I want to feel like I did the night Phoebe let me borrow her clothes, but I don't want to be borrowing someone else's style and life. I want to be my own kind of super.

I've seen enough movies and TV shows to know that there's only one way to solve this: a makeover montage. I wonder if Phoebe can take me to the mall.

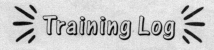

Training Log

Lindsay's Makeover List:

New glasses

Skinny jeans and/or leggings

Cool shirts: Maybe it's time to ditch the cartoons and get some
more grown-up tops? I mean, Batgirl doesn't wear a shirt
with Supergirl's face on it. That would be weird.

Canvas backpack

Better hair (?)

Ever evolving,

Lindsay

(I kinda like this one!)

CHAPTER 15

"You know a makeover montage doesn't just happen, right? Music isn't going to start playing at the store, and we might not even find an outfit," Phoebe says as she pours her coffee while I sit at the counter the next morning. I was up late last night listing what I needed in my makeover shopping list. Now that I'm listing it out to Phoebe at the breakfast bar, it does seem a little extreme. But desperate times call for desperate measures.

"I know, I know," I say impatiently. "But can we go to the mall anyway?"

"Of course," she says. "After we practice your front and rear wheel lifts. And we will find the perfect outfit, I promise. We'll even blast some music so it feels like a montage."

I roll my eyes, but just between us, I'm ridiculously excited to practice with my new bike, and I actually trust Phoebe when she says we'll find the right outfit. Ten minutes later, the breakfast dishes are in the dishwasher and Phoebe and I are in the driveway. I'm riding directly at a curb, and every time I get within a few inches of it, I swerve out of the way. Phoebe, on the other hand, is riding next to me, and every time we get to the curb, she gently lifts her front wheel up by leaning her weight back; then once she's up, she pushes her weight forward so the rear wheel gently follows. It's like she's not even pedaling over an obstacle at all, just hovering. Like she has secret jet packs in her bike, or helium in her tires. Hmmm . . .

"I know it looks scary now," she says sympathetically. I must look pretty pathetic. "It took me months to get over a curb the first time," she says. That makes me feel a little better, and I attempt to bring my front wheel off the ground, yanking the bars up. I feel the slightest bit of lift and immediately slam back down, convinced I've come a heartbeat from toppling backward.

Phoebe looks like she wants to giggle, but she doesn't. Instead, she suggests we move to the grass for a little while. I'm not sure if it's because I'm just that bad or because I'm so obviously terrified, but I'm grateful either way. She goes inside and comes out with a backpack that's completely packed—it's going to be way too heavy to wear while riding. But when she hands it over to me, it feels almost weightless. "I stuffed it with a pillow," she explains. "Now you don't have to worry about tipping over."

I don't know exactly how that's supposed to make it easier—I can't help picturing myself landing and looking like a turtle. But she directs me to ride at a stick lying on the ground and try to lift my front wheel over it by shifting my hips and my weight back so I can let the front wheel "just come off the ground."

I feel a little more in control as I roll at it, and the stick is coming up as I pedal. "And . . . lift!" Phoebe shouts, and before I realize what I'm doing, I'm giving a little tug—not a yank—and shifting backward, and the wheel does lift, just a tiny bit, and comes down right on the other side of the stick.

"I did it!" I shout. "And I didn't fall over!"

Phoebe high-fives me, and I've never felt so cool—and not just because I made contact on the high five. We do a few more repetitions of that, riding over the stick again and again. I haven't quite gotten the rear wheel part of it, but by the end of the thirty minutes I promised Phoebe I'd work, I've gotten the front wheel up eight times in a row, which she says is good progress.

"Before we head to the mall, I think there's one more thing you should agree to if we're doing this makeover," she says as we pedal back toward the house. "I think you should think about entering that jump competition I know you stole the flyer for."

I almost fall over. "I can't do a competition!" I say,

maybe a little too loud. The old guy next door walking his dog gives me a dirty look. Definitely too loud.

"Then why did you grab the flyer?" Phoebe asks. Darn her and her logic!

"I . . . Well, I was maybe thinking about it, considering it, tossing the idea around, contemplating it," I babble a little desperately.

"There are beginner categories, so it won't be like you're racing against pros," Phoebe says. "You don't have to say yes right away. I just want you to think about it."

"I promise I'll think about it," I say, crossing my fingers behind my back. Some things are just too scary.

"All right, kid," she says, pushing her bike into the house. "Let's go shopping. You have your mom's credit card, right?"

"Do you think it'll be okay if I use it?" I ask. "I have a hundred dollars that she gave me for spending money."

"I texted her this morning. She says it's cool as long as we don't pierce your nose." She pauses, looking at me critically. "But you would look cute with a little stud."

I laugh nervously. "We're not actually going to . . ."

"Pierce your nose? Not a chance."

Training Log

I take back what I said about getting over the stick in the grass being the coolest I've ever felt. The mall with Phoebe is way, way cooler. And at the same time, way, way scarier than any curb I need to ride over.

> **Superhero Tip:** Be careful what you wish for, because your cousin may end up taking you shopping.

Again, I fear this might be my last journal entry.

Written from the food court,
Lindsay
(That one stinks, but I am full of fries and don't care.)

CHAPTER 16

We walk quickly past all the kids' stores I usually shop at, and I'm starting to regret writing the list that I showed to Phoebe. It's getting more and more nerve-racking as we pass cooler and cooler stores and people. "Maybe we should just go home," I start to say, when she stops in front of a skate shop.

She looks right at home, in jeans ripped at the knees and a black tank top that shows off the very top of her tattoo, plus a bulky silver watch on her right arm. A beat-up leather backpack is over her shoulder, and her hair is pulled back in a tiny bun that she tossed up in the car. She looks like a rock star. I'm wearing practically the same thing—minus the tattoo—but my baggy jeans and purple T-shirt make me look like I'm a little kid, not a rock star, even though we're almost the same height.

"This is our first spot," she says. "You need new shoes if you're going to ride."

"Good," I say. I take a deep breath. Maybe she won't notice that I've been holding it in. "I knew that."

We walk in, and I'm surrounded by shoes I've never seen before. Mom always buys mine from whatever department store she's in when I outgrow my old ones. I've never had to pick them out myself.

"Which ones should I get?" I ask Phoebe, who's already standing over a pair of slip-on sneakers. They're made from a shiny black snakeskin material and have dark gray soles. They look like a cross between old and new Phoebe—tough and kind of scary, but still really athletic.

"I love these," she mumbles, like she didn't even hear me. She looks up. "Sorry, did you say something?" She grins. "Shoe shopping. It gets me every time. But what about these for you? You need a shoe with a firm enough sole that it won't be bending over your pedals when you ride." She picks up a pair of plain black canvas shoes with the same dark gray sole. They're not as outrageous as the ones she's hugging under one arm for herself, and they seem just right for me. Not too loud, but not exactly quiet either.

A sales assistant helps me find the right size, and they're comfortable enough that I want to get out and walk around the mall in them. "Done," I say, grabbing them.

"We haven't even started," Phoebe says, glancing over her shoulder as she marches down the aisle toward the register. "Don't you know how to shop? It's a marathon, not a sprint," she warns me as I run to catch up. These shoes don't seem to really go with what I'm wearing, but if I were to make a guess, I think Phoebe is dead set on changing that in the immediate future. Suddenly, my long list of things I need is starting to seem a little more intimidating than fun. (This might be one of those "be careful what you wish for" moments that my mom warned me about.)

We walk out of that store and directly into the one next to it, where the walls are decorated with skateboards. "I thought I was getting stuff for bike riding," I whisper, trying to stay cool.

"BMX and skateboarding are really similar in style," Phoebe explains. "And a lot of kids do both. But cycling is better," she says in a low voice, glancing around to make sure no one heard her. She goes over to a shelf of jeans. "Jeans are on your list, right?" I nod. "You'll want a couple of pairs that fit a little bit better than what you have. I'm not just saying that for fashion reasons, though there's that too. But if they're tighter in the legs, you won't catch them in the chain of your bike." She grabs a couple of dark blue and black pairs. "I don't know about black jeans for you, but you can try them on," she says.

"Why not?" I ask. "Am I not cool enough?"

She gets a funny look on her face. "No, kiddo," she says. "I just mean . . . Look. At your age, girls aren't always nice to you, right?" I nod again. "Sometimes, it's hard to really stand out and do your own thing. I just don't want you to end up with clothes that will make you feel uncomfortable. I got picked on a lot when I was your age for wearing lots of black and super-punk stuff."

"Do you wish you'd been different?" I ask, not really

sure if I want to know the answer. "I mean, more normal," I clarify, but somehow that seems even worse.

Instead of getting grumpy, her face lights up. "Not in a million years . . . Even if it drove my mom crazy." She grabs a few thin, dark gray sweaters off a nearby rack, and a black tank top to go with them. She hands them over and marches me to the dressing room.

I swap my loose jeans for the skinny black pair, shove on my new shoes, and drag on the tank top and the sweater, which hangs slightly off my shoulder and shows off the straps of the tank top. A hat comes sailing over the door—a black flat-brimmed baseball cap that says "Joyride" in big white cursive letters.

"Put that on!" she shouts. I do, and I stare in the mirror. I look pretty cool, to be honest. The black and gray doesn't look like how any of the other girls at school dress, but it feels pretty punk rock—in a way that I can totally handle. And the hat makes me feel like I actually belong on the tracks at Joyride, not just on the sidelines.

"I love it," I whisper, doing a twirl. I've never wanted to twirl in a new outfit before. "It's definitely not pink."

"Let me see!" Phoebe says, banging on the door. I open it and grin, and her face widens into a smile as she snaps a picture and texts someone.

"You look amazing!" she says, high-fiving me. "Maybe you can pull off black pants."

"And if I can't, who cares?" I say boldly.

Her phone pings. Whoever she texted must have been waiting for her message. "Your mom says you look fabulous, and she's so excited that her baby is growing up," Phoebe says, reading off her phone.

"You sent her a picture?" I ask, slightly horrified.

"She is paying for it," Phoebe responds.

"Tell her . . . thanks, I guess," I say. And it is pretty cool that my mom's on board with this makeover, even though it's to kind of undo the style she's forced on me for years. Why is black and gray okay now? If I'd known I just needed to be nicer to Phoebe to dress cooler, I would have talked to her a long time ago and gotten this shopping trip on the road.

"How did you get my mom to agree to this?" I ask.

"Honestly? Your mom thought she was putting you in stylish clothes and that you'd be wearing what the other kids in school were wearing," Phoebe says. "She was trying—but you've seen pictures of her and my mom as teenagers. They're not the most fashion-forward."

She's got that right.

But we're not here to complain about my mom's terrible acid-wash jeans. (Not right now anyway.)

"Find me another outfit!" I say, running back to the dressing room. Black leggings come flying in, along with a sporty, dark purple dress. They're followed by dark blue jeans and a purple T-shirt with a small white pocket, and a dark gray vest with lime-green piping that looks like something Mom would have worn in the nineties.

"Seriously?" I say.

"You wanted a makeover, didn't you?" Phoebe asks innocently. "And this does match your bike pretty perfectly. We're going for a theme here, you know."

Weirdly enough, the vest looks cool with the T-shirt under it. And it really will match with my bike!

With a huge pile of clothes (and the Joyride hat—how cool is it that the shop stocks Joyride merchandise?), we head to the cash register and Phoebe hands over the credit card again.

"Time to go home?" I ask.

"Kid, you're really new to the makeover thing, aren't you?" Phoebe replies. "We still haven't hit the big stuff."

Five minutes later, we're standing outside an eyeglass store. "No, no, no, no!" I say. "No contacts, I don't care how many makeovers require them."

"No one thinks you should get contacts," Phoebe says, rolling her eyes. "We're here for glasses." We walk in, and she goes straight to a pair of glasses in the back. Rectangular and with thick black frames, but they seem small enough that they won't look goofy and oversized on me. "Try these on." She shoves them into my hands and plucks my current wire-rims off my nose.

I always wanted thick black frames, but Mom said they

were too much like the ones she hated when she was a kid, so she wanted me to get invisible rims instead. The compromise was getting the wire-rimmed glasses—more nerdy than cool librarian, and I've been stuck with them for years.

When I tried on the black frames during our last shopping trip, though, I actually felt super—like I could rip them off and suddenly fly, Superman-style, if I had to. They made me look intellectual, but also like I maybe played in a rock band on the weekends (which is the look I'd be going for if I had a choice).

I slide on the frames and glance in the mirror. I was afraid I'd look nerdy, but instead, I look like Clark Kent, the mild-mannered reporter. I look . . . kind of cool.

"I love them!" I exclaim. It's almost too easy. These are the glasses I've wanted for so long. I know that comic book characters totally change their appearance with glasses, but who knew it would work on me, in real life?

Phoebe puts in the order for them with my prescription.

"Last stop," Phoebe says, and pulls me into another store. I don't think I've ever shopped this much in my life.

We emerge a few minutes later with a purple canvas backpack, which Phoebe says will break up all the black and keep me from looking like a cat burglar. I tried arguing for all black, like Catwoman, but she just laughed and said my mom might not appreciate that.

"What about jewelry?" I ask, suddenly panicked.

"You can borrow a few things from me and see what you like," Phoebe says. "Geez, I've created a monster."

I shoot her a look. "Not literally!" she laughs. No potions or secret magic spells, just the power of a good shopping trip.

"And, Linds," she says, pausing midwalk. "I am cutting your hair when we get home. . . . After we go meet Ali at Joyride."

Eep.

Training Log

Sitting in the car and glancing in the mirror, I already feel different, just from the new outfit and the subtle changes that Phoebe has made to my hair. It's in a side braid, since it got a little frizzy from all the on-and-off when trying on clothes. I like it, and I'm almost feeling excited to see the girls at Joyride again. But not quite yet. I do kind of want that haircut, now that Phoebe explained what she wants to do, and I'm still a little nervous. It feels a little like I'm playing dress-up as a cool skater girl, not actually someone who's good at tricks and being . . . cool.

> **Superhero Tip:** I think—and I need to investigate this further—that maybe the trick to looking cool is confidence. Wearing almost the same thing as Phoebe, I still don't feel as cool as her, but I worry that might be because I'm not owning it. And I'm not totally sure how.

Dorkily yours,
Lindsay
(Still accurate, regardless of clothing choices.)

CHAPTER 17

Before we go home so Phoebe can take scissors to my hair, we head to Joyride. I almost forgot that Ali and I had made that four p.m. riding plan, but Phoebe had it in her calendar, and since we're running early, we even have time to ride together before I have to start being social. So I can ease into it.

Of course, "ease in" is pushing it, since inside, it's kid-filled chaos. Music is blaring, and a boy skids to a stop inches from hitting me. He just nods and rolls off while I stand there shaking. Phoebe goes behind the desk, says hi to a few people who are waving to her, and grabs an envelope. Then she walks back to me.

"You know what you need?"

I'm afraid to find out.

"You need to nail a move," she says, ignoring the look on my face as she plunks a helmet on my head. "If you can get one trick, the rest get a lot easier. Trust me."

I don't know that I totally believe her, but she might have a point. "Can I do that?" I ask, pointing at a couple of kids who can't be more than six years old, who are riding toward a small plank on the floor at top speed, then lifting their wheels over it so they don't hit it.

"A bunny hop?" she says, following my gaze. "Sure,

why not? It's just a bit more advanced than what you've already done in the yard."

We find a back party room that's been partied out, with streamers hanging limp and popcorn kernels all over the floor. With the door shut, it's a little quieter. Phoebe points to a line on the floor. "That's your plank," she says.

"I thought I had to jump over something tall?" I ask, confused. Last I looked, the guys out there talking about bunny hopping were going over really big stuff.

"Well, yeah," Phoebe says. "But you need to walk before you run, grasshopper."

For some reason I find this utterly hilarious, and I get a bad case of the giggles. But that doesn't stop Phoebe from pointing to the line again. "The goal is to ride at the line, pull your front wheel up and over, and then as you get that wheel over and onto the ground again, lift the rear wheel."

I got lost around "front wheel up," so I just stare blankly at her.

"It's just a smoother version of what we worked on this morning," she says. "You're just putting it all together."

She grabs her bike and stands over it. "Pretend you're Supergirl. You're flying and there's a building right in front of you. You'd pull your arms up a little and the rest of your body would follow, and your arms would go up and over the building first. Then when your arms tilt back down, your legs would lift over it and then tilt back down. Make sense?"

That sounds more like something I can get behind. I grab my bike, feeling a little more confident (and just a little more super). I take a few pedals, then try to get the front wheel to lift.

"One, two, three, lift," I mutter to myself, but the wheel stays firmly planted on the ground. I repeat the process again, and again, but each time, my wheel refuses to lift.

"Stop thinking about the second part and just focus on the first," Phoebe calls helpfully. (It's not really that helpful. I can't stop focusing on both parts.)

"One, two, thre—"

"BOO!" Phoebe shrieks, and I'm so startled that I jump a little backward, moving my whole body, not just yanking the bike with my arms like I've been trying to do. And miraculously, the front wheel lifts off the ground, way more than it did with the stick earlier today.

"I did it!" I shriek back, and Phoebe cracks up.

"Okay, now do it again," she smirks. I push my sleeves up and check my helmet, then pedal at the line on the floor, concentrating hard. As it gets closer, I tense my whole body like I'm about to get scared again, and when the crack is right in front of me, I let the tension go, using it to lift me upward, and I feel my front wheel pull off the ground for a heartbeat. It's not a big leap, but it's definitely off the ground. And as the front wheel taps back down, I push my weight forward and try to loosen up so the back wheel pops—just the tiniest bit—off the floor, following me like Supergirl up and over a building.

Phoebe claps and cheers, and turns up the volume on the stereo system in the room so loud music blasts out. "Let's keep going!" she shouts.

"What are we listening to?" I yell back. She looks shocked.

"You haven't ever listened to the Ramones?" she asks, and seems completely taken aback. When I shake my head, she shakes hers too and under her breath grumbles, "Man, we have a lot of work to do. They're classic punk!"

"Classic punk. Lift the wheel. Hold tension," I whisper to myself as I face down the line again. Sometimes, being the younger cousin stinks.

Jen pops her head in the door right as I hit the move again—still not getting too high, but getting a little smoother now. "Wow," she says, looking almost impressed. "That was pretty good, for a beginner."

Phoebe doesn't realize I'm looking at her, and I see her roll her eyes. "Jen," she says, "how long have you been here today?"

"My grandparents dropped me off this morning," Jen says, tossing her hair and rolling all the way into the room. "I wanted to practice some tricks for that competition."

"You know, you can't learn to do big jumps all in one day," Phoebe says, looking concerned. "That's how you get hurt."

"I'm fine," Jen snaps.

"Okay," says Phoebe. "Just don't forget to get some good rest time too. And have fun while you're here! Are you riding with anyone today?"

"I wanted to work solo this time," Jen says stubbornly. "I really want to win that gold frame in the competition."

"Are you sure? We're just going to keep working on making Lindsay's bunny hop better for a bit, if you want to join us. And Ali is going to be here soon."

Jen smiles just a little and says she might swing by for a bit to get a break. But when she rides away, I see her looking back at us and I wonder if she wants to train solo for the same reasons I would—not because I don't like her, but because being around other girls makes me sort of want to hide under the covers and read a book instead. I think Phoebe might have had a point about Jen being just as scared of me as I am of her. And in my new jeans and sweater, I feel pretty fabulous—I'd be intimidated by me!

Soon after Jen pedals off, Phoebe

drags me to the front to meet Ali, who's right on time. She waves and smiles, then rolls over to us.

"You look great!" she says to me. "I love your outfit!"

"Thanks." I grin. "Yours too." She looks funky in her skinny jeans and big flannel shirt, and her red hair is popping out from under the helmet.

"Phoebe, we're going to go hit the jump line—do you want to come?" Ali asks.

"You girls go ahead, I'll meet you there," Phoebe says, and before I can say a word, she's already rolling away. I'm alone, backed into a be-friendly corner. So I bravely smile and together, Ali and I pedal over to the smallest of the jump lines.

Within two runs, I'm realizing two key things: first, trying to jump is absolutely exhausting. Every part of me is tired. But, second, it's not unlike doing a bunny hop—the motion is almost the exact same; you're just trying to pump the bike over the top of a jump instead of over

a stick on the ground. It's starting to make a little more sense.

After the third time through the lineup of five two-foot-high bumps, Ali and I both stop to catch our breath.

"I think I definitely got air on that last one," I say.

"Yeah, for sure," Ali says, but my superhero senses detect that she might just be humoring me.

"Okay, it wasn't much air, exactly, but still!" I exclaim.

"Very impressive, yes," she says, and starts laughing.

As she's laughing, Jen rides up. "What's so funny?" she asks.

"Oh, we were just talking about the awesome job Lindsay just did on the jump line," Ali says, suddenly looking totally serious.

"Really?" Jen looks skeptical.

Phoebe picks just then to roll back to us and skids to a stop right at the top of the jump line. Perfect timing.

"You girls ready to really get to work?" she asks, raising an eyebrow.

We all nod and look at each other nervously. Finally, Jen and I are on the same page.

"Come on, let's get moving," Phoebe says, and like a line of baby ducks behind the mommy duck, we fall in behind her and pedal.

⋛ Training Log ⋚

We spent the next hour practicing over and over, and by the end, Jen and I were both pretty good at getting over the line on the floor. We graduated to a tiny board that's only about an inch high— but we both managed to clear it without touching it, which Phoebe said is great progress.

Superhero Tip: (1) Tiny pieces of progress will add up in bike skills, so that tiny board will become a big jump if I keep working. And (2) even if you're a fast rider like Jen, you might not be great at skills. She can go a million times faster than me, but she's only a little better on the bunny hop.

Progressively,
Lindsay
(Meh.)

CHAPTER 18

"Should we invite Jen and Ali over to hang out tonight, maybe even have a sleepover?" Phoebe asks me in a low voice as we start heading to leave our bikes in Phoebe's office so we don't need to bring them in and out of the van tonight.

"Sure," I say, trying to act casual, but my heartbeat has sped up to warp speed and I'm sure I'm about to pass out. What if they don't want to come over? What if they do want to come over? It's my first sleepover—I can't be expected to handle it well!

(I know what you're thinking: How have I never had a sleepover, at twelve years old? The honest answer? By avoiding it like the plague. Mom is always suggesting that I invite girls over, but there aren't really any girls in school I would want to hang out with for that long. I don't think so anyway. What would I talk about for that many hours?)

I'm pretty sure the whole bike park has started to move around in circles; that's how dizzy with nerves I'm starting to feel about this plan.

"Jen! Ali!" Phoebe calls before I can grab her and tell her I've changed my mind, that I just want to go home and watch cartoons in my room with Penguin curled up on his pillow next to me. But Jen is already riding over, looking bored and effortlessly cool.

Before I know it, Jen and Ali are with Phoebe and they're chatting away. They all seem so comfortable with each other that I'm feeling left out.

"Linds!" Jen shouts, smiling at me. "Are you into getting takeout at the Mexican place for dinner?" She doesn't look like she's dreading spending time with me, and that means Phoebe has already sold her on the slumber party. I feel myself start to smile—and remember Phoebe's advice that Jen is probably just as nervous being around us. I mean, considering Phoebe is my cousin and I was nervous around her until this week, I do understand that feeling pretty well.

"I'm always into getting good Mexican food," I say.

"A lot of our family moved here from Mexico," Phoebe informs my new friend, "and Lindsay's taste in food is fantastic—so she's a pro at picking the best stuff on the menu. Want to let her do the ordering?"

"Absolutely!" says Jen, more enthusiastic than I've ever seen her. Score—I think I have a new friend!

The pressure is on, but this is my time to shine— I know the best place in town, and they know how to make the perfect tacos (that don't get messy and spill everywhere). I order in fluent Spanish, and Ali and Jen both seem awed by that. It's not that big a deal, but I did make a pretty excellent order: my favorite carnitas tacos with extra avocado slices and lime wedges on the side. I forget that not everyone speaks another language, though, because when I finish ordering with a "gracias," I see that Jen and Ali are staring at me with their mouths hanging open.

"What?" I ask.

"How did you learn that?" Ali says.

"Speaking Spanish?"

She nods.

"My whole family speaks Spanish," I say. "I've been hearing it since I was a baby, so I guess it's just always been something I knew, like how you learn to speak English."

"That is *so* cool," Jen says enthusiastically, and she seems genuine about it. "I wish I could speak another language!"

They make me start teaching them Spanish phrases like it's a really exciting, new thing for them, and seem shocked when I explain that I grew up switching between Spanish and English at home.

We end up with a van full of tacos and tortilla chips with spicy guacamole, plus some flan for dessert. My mouth is watering. As soon as we get home, we dig into our tacos in Phoebe's kitchen while we talk about the upcoming jump competition. Ali is excited about it too, and Phoebe keeps staring me down like she knows I'm going to cave and sign up.

"There's a *gold* bike frame that you can win," Ali says,

almost dropping her taco in her excitement. "Haven't you noticed Jen staring at it as you walk into the park? It's right there on display."

Jen, of course, is in. She tells us again that she's already done a ton of racing on the road. She's trying to sound casual, but she seems more flustered than usual and a lot less excited than I would have expected from someone so competitive. It seems like she has a pretty love/hate relationship with the idea of racing.

"If you love racing so much, why did your parents make you stop this summer?" Ali asks.

"They just thought it was time I took a break," Jen says defensively.

"Okay, why did you need a break?" Ali is definitely prying a little bit here, but Jen looks like she's struggling between wanting to tell us about it and wanting to keep it to herself. But talking wins out.

"I was starting to feel really bad every time I started a race—like I was going to throw up, or pass out, or both. I almost dropped my bike and ran away at the last one . . . but I couldn't stop signing up for them," she admits. "Finally, my parents told me no more races, after I freaked out and threw my bike at the end of the last one."

"Whoa," says Phoebe. "That's an intense reaction. I've only ever seen one other guy do that!"

"What happened?" Ali asks.

"I didn't win," Jen says, like that's the obvious reason

for someone to throw a bike. (Phoebe would kill me if I so much as dropped mine too hard!) Even her telling us that seemed really hard for her, and Ali and I just listen quietly as she keeps talking about how badly she wanted to win. It seems crazy to me, but I guess it's similar to how I feel when I don't get an A on a writing assignment. . . . I do not throw my computer, though.

"I just couldn't stop thinking about what happened at the end of that race. I wanted to ride my bike, but I hated my bike," she says. She gets really quiet after she says that, and even though the image of her throwing her bike in a temper tantrum is kind of funny, it does seem like she's had some issues with being too competitive.

"So just to be clear, you do know throwing your bike is a bad move, right?" asks Phoebe, and Jen nods.

"My parents were pretty upset—and it was super embarrassing afterward," Jen adds.

It's not just Jen who has some problems with racing, apparently. Ali has also raced a few times, but hated that her older brothers were unimpressed with her finishes in the small women's fields. "I mean, I can't help how few girls are in my races!" she says, gesturing angrily with a tortilla chip.

"You girls need to get back to the fun of racing," Phoebe says, popping into the conversation and handing out glasses of her fresh-brewed kombucha, which I sip tentatively and Ali slurps down. Jen sniffs it daintily, takes a small sip, and almost spits it out. "It's an acquired taste," Phoebe says apologetically as Jen silently hands her glass to Ali.

"Fun of racing?" Jen asks suspiciously.

"Yeah—racing can be awesome in the right environment," Phoebe says. "It sounds like you got way more serious about it than you should have. Race results aren't who you are; they're just numbers. And as for you, Ali, if what your brothers think matters more than how you feel at the end of the race, you're not enjoying the race enough to bother with it. That's why this jumping competition might be good for all of you," she adds, looking right at me. "It's short, it's fun, it's no-pressure, there's a party after—and there isn't a start line to get sick on while surrounded by a pack of kids. And since it's skill-based, we can have you all doing awesome jumps. So?"

She looks around the table. Jen is the first to speak, and to no one's surprise, she's going to do the competition. "I really do miss racing," she says, "but I don't think I want to race on the road bike anytime soon. So I'm in."

Ali smiles. "Me too."

She puts her hand out in the middle of the circle we've formed, and Jen slaps hers right on top.

That leaves me. All three of them are staring. Phoebe looks hopeful, and Jen looks curious, like she's not sure if I'll have the guts or not. Ali nods at me encouragingly.

"Fine," I say, clearly outnumbered, and put my hand in on top of Jen's.

For a shining second, we all cheer loudly but I know we're all still nervous, each of us for different reasons. Phoebe reaches over and pats me on the back. "It'll be painless, I promise," she whispers. I smile weakly at her— I want to believe that's true, but while I might be able to handle another crash on the bike, the idea of being in front of a bunch of judges and my new friends still seems pretty painful to me.

"Okay, enough about the competition," Ali says, interrupting my train of thought. "Lindsay, what do you do when you're not riding bikes?"

"I haven't really been riding bikes that long," I say. "And until last week, I mainly read for fun. Which I still do."

"Sure, but what do you like reading?" Ali asks, standing up to refill her water glass and stretch her long legs.

I reach over to my backpack and pull out the latest Wonder Woman issue that I've been going through. "I just started this one, and it's great."

"That's awesome!" Jen says, grabbing it from me. "I love her bracelets. And Wonder Woman is one of my favorites."

Jen clearly has some hidden depths. "I didn't know you were into comic books," I say. "Isn't it kind of nerdy?"

"Are you kidding?" she says, smiling. "Wonder Woman is so cool! Think about everything she can do."

"Yeah, I know," I say. "I've been reading comic books for years. I don't think it's nerdy, but I figured you would."

"No way! Have you seen the Wonder Woman animated movie?" she asks enthusiastically. I nod, still slightly shell-shocked that this super-cool girl likes the same thing I do. "It was great, right?"

I nod again. "Phoebe has it, if you want to watch it again," I add. (I know we just watched it the other night, but honestly, I could rewatch it a million times. And who am I kidding? I already have rewatched it a ton.)

"I haven't seen it and I'd be into it," Ali says, sitting back down. "But, Jen, I didn't know you were a closet comic nerd."

"It's true," she says, grinning.

Phoebe stands up. "While it's tempting to watch the movie with you yet again, I have some work I should do. . . . But I'll make you guys some popcorn; you earned it today."

While she buzzes around the kitchen making movie snacks, we lay out some sleeping bags on the living room floor so we can watch in comfort as Penguin meanders around us, sniffing at pillows, socks, and Ali's and Jen's backpacks. He plops down by my pillow (I knew he'd still like me best!), and we settle into our sleeping bags as the opening credits roll.

Training Log

I woke up this morning feeling a slight sense of dread. Why, why, why did I agree to enter a competition? Me!? I don't compete, unless it's a challenge for who can read the most books. (Me. I can.) This is madness. I'm not ready for this! I can't get ready for this! I don't know how the other girls are still asleep, and not panicking. I forgot about the competition as we watched the movie last night, but it hit me again right when the sun rose this morning and I've been freaking out ever since. Jen is snoring softly (ha!) while Ali is curled into a tiny ball in her sleeping bag—they didn't even wake up when I slipped out of mine and got up to write at the table! I don't wanna. Penguin, however, is scratching at my pillow, so I must end this journal entry and seek solace in dachshund snuggles instead.

> **Superhero Tip:** Probably don't commit to things when you're under the influence of tacos and inspirational movies. . . . Or maybe that's the best time to commit to things?

Woof,
Penguin (and Lindsay)
(That's not going to last.)

CHAPTER 19

After a quick breakfast of granola and yogurt, Phoebe loads us right back into the van and drives to Joyride for an early session.

"Okay, girls. Today we're going to conquer the pump track," Phoebe says to Jen, Ali, and me. We're perched on a platform in front of a small wooden oval that has waves of wood three feet high. The point, as far as I can tell as I watch other kids sprint around it, is to pedal off the platform into the first hump, then somehow go faster and faster as they go around the thirty-second loop without pedaling. They seem to be moving their bodies more than their legs; it's like a weird ballet.

"Those bumps are called whoops," Phoebe explains. "And those turns, the ones that are slightly banked up the side so you're a bit tilted, those are called berms."

She explains that we want to focus on our body position and keep ourselves low to the bike, not coasting, while we stand straight up. Our elbows and knees should be bent, and before she lets us grab our bikes, she makes us stand like that for a while on the platform. It feels a little silly.

"Why don't they pedal?" I ask, looking at the riders who are already ripping around the track.

"Great question!" Phoebe says. "It's awesome that you noticed that. The key to riding a pump track well isn't pedaling, although getting a bit of speed to start is a good thing. It's all about moving your whole body with the bike," she explains.

She rolls away and into the tiny jump line to demonstrate. It's technically for little kids to play on next to the pump track, with little six-inch-high rollers, but she doesn't seem deterred by that. Luckily, there are no speedy three-year-olds around. After she takes a couple of pedal strokes, she starts using her arms intensely, pushing down when she's going down the slight declines, and almost pulling as she goes up the tiny inclines.

"It's about timing your pressure into the ground over those rolls so you propel yourself forward," she says, riding back to us. "So what we're going to do is practice feeling where you want to push down, and when you want to let go and let the bike come up a bit."

"Okay, say all of that again but in English," Jen says, and for the first time, I find her sarcasm both hilarious and helpful. Ali looks just as perplexed.

We're clearly all a little confused, so Phoebe tries again. "If I push you on a swing and you're just sitting, you're not going to go forever. You'll slow down pretty quick. But you can do things, like swing your legs or push into the chain with your hands, and you'll keep swinging forever even with a tiny push to start. The tiny push here is that initial pedaling, and if you move right, you'll be doing almost the same thing you would on the swing."

It's starting to make sense. Ali and Jen are nodding, though they look nervous too. Jen, of course, volunteers to go first. She pedals a few revolutions and heads down onto the oval. She hits the first hump and sails smoothly over it. She goes over the other side, sets up for the next bump, and, as she heads up, starts to pedal. The pedal clips the top of the bump, knocking her off balance, and she skids slightly, makes it down, but veers off the oval track and comes to a stop. She looks a little defeated, but she's not cursing or shouting, so that's a plus.

Ali looks terrified now that Jen didn't make it, but she gamely pedals down and onto the oval. She makes it over two humps before she pedals and does the same thing Jen did—she almost saves it but rolls off the course and over to where Jen stopped on the side of the track. The two are standing there, waving me on.

"Just remember not to pedal once you're going over the bumps, even if it feels like you have to," Phoebe whispers to me.

I start pedaling and drop onto the track. The first bump looms ahead of me. I close my eyes and feel my muscles tighten up, but then feel a bit of a whoosh of air as I start down the back. I made it! My muscles relax, but

I don't have time to even consider pedaling before I'm already up and over the second. The same thing happens on the third.

The fourth one, though, I see coming, and I feel like I don't have enough speed to make it over, so against Phoebe's suggestions, I try to pedal, and immediately clip the pedal on the wood and end up scooting down the backside out of control and off the course.

Ali and Jen ride up to me. "You did great!" Ali says, while Jen—who, judging by her expression, clearly expected to do the best—just nods and smiles tightly. Meanwhile, I'm stunned. "How did you get over the third bump?" Ali asks enthusiastically.

"Fear, mostly. And I kept my eyes shut at first," I say honestly, shrugging.

"Maybe don't try that as a tactic," Phoebe says, rolling up to the three of us. "But Linds did do a couple of things that I didn't even really explain . . . even if they were by accident." She nudges me with her hip playfully, so I know she's actually pretty proud. "So let's go again."

Ali and Jen race each other to the starting drop-in, while I pedal back next to Phoebe. "I really did okay?" I ask.

"You did awesome. But next time, try to keep your eyes open the whole time! Trust me, you never want to hit a jump blind," she says. "And remember that tense feeling when all your muscles tighten up when you're nervous? That's sort of like how it should feel when you push down—and then, when you're going up, pretend that you're floating. Relax at the top, and then do it all again."

"Tension. I can do tension," I mutter, mostly to myself. "I'm great at tension."

"Tell me about it," Phoebe says, and I think she gets what I mean—being tensed up and tight is kind of my natural posture on the bike still. We do what feels like hundreds of laps, and by the end, we're almost all the way around without pedaling. Phoebe explains that a pedal stroke occasionally isn't a bad thing, but shows us how to do it when we're between the bumps—never when we're on one.

And after a few slips, Jen is smooth. "It's easy once you get it the first time," she says casually—but I saw her hand quivering a tiny bit before she started that run. Ali already mostly figured out the technique, and is trying to jump and actually get air over the bumps. Me? I'm just focusing on getting Phoebe's push-and-float method down and doing it every single time.

As we're all walking out, the girls run ahead to meet their rides at the front. Phoebe tells me I did really well.

"I don't think I did that great," I admit. "I was feeling okay and wasn't scared by the end, but I wasn't getting in the air like Ali was."

"Yeah, but did you notice that when she did that, she wasn't pushing, she was pulling?" Phoebe asks. "Later, that's going to slow her down. You focused on learning the basic technique, and that's how you get good. That's rule number one when you're working with me, and with any good coach."

Hmm.

Training Log

It's been a couple of days, but I'm back and about to go practice on the pump track by myself. It's early in the day, and we came in before the park opened so that Phoebe could get some work done in the office. She doesn't just work with Ali, Jen, and me, she explained today: she helps manage the park and coaches on the side—not just the three of us—and apparently she's in pretty high demand.

~~~~~~~~~~

She's way busier than I realized. When we walked in, the guy who I think owns the whole park practically fainted with relief that she was there to help him with something, and she's been in the office on her computer for way longer than I think she expected. I already read for a while, ate breakfast, and practiced on the pump track— I'm on a break now, since Phoebe says the worst time to practice is when you're already tired.

> **Superhero Tip:** Resting is just as important as riding if you want to get better. Phoebe hasn't gotten to ride or rest yet, and I can see her face going from early morning still-sleepy to straight-up grumpy.

It's time for me to head back out, even though I'm still a little bit sleepy. I don't want to wake the beast, or she might really turn into a supervillain!

Feeling sluggish,
Lindsay
(That's not inspiring.)

CHAPTER 20

The park is open and buzzing with kids, but it's not as scary as before—instead, I relish the feeling of being one of the cool ones who get to practice before it's even open. As I'm taking another quick break from going around and around the track (and getting a little dizzy after quite a few rounds), Dave—the cute boy I met last week—skids to a stop in front of me. I have a half second to note how happy I am that I'm wearing my new dark blue jeans and the fitted purple T-shirt with the white pocket, plus my new shoes. Phoebe finally harassed me into trimming my hair, and it's now just a little longer than shoulder length—though you can't tell today, since it's in a French braid. But the big change is bangs, which help highlight the best part of my outfit: the new glasses, which came in yesterday.

"So are you going to do the competition?" he asks, without so much as a hello. All anyone's been talking about is this competition, though, so I'm not surprised.

Either way—he's talking to me! But also . . . yikes: competing. "Phoebe signed me up, but I'm just not sure I want to do any kind of competition. I'm not very competitive. At least, I never have been. I've never competed," I reply. I blush realizing I probably should have played that a little cooler; he didn't need my life story. Or for me to repeat the word "compete" so many times. For someone who writes a lot, my vocabulary is not so good with the talking and the words.

"Why not? You've been doing great on the pump track. I saw your bunny hop practice earlier today, and you're getting a lot better."

"Sure, but I'm still not that good," I reply. "And what if I fall? Or don't get any air on the jump line?" That's what I'm really nervous about. It's not a competition for who can bunny hop a line on the ground. I'll need to combine what I've been doing on the pump track with the bunny hop motion and try to actually sail over those bumps, which will be bigger than anything I've been practicing on so far.

"So you fall. Who cares?" he says, pushing his hair back. Man, he's cute. Behind him, Phoebe rides by and mouths something at me. I think it was "Act casual." She's followed by Jen, who points at Dave and gives me a thumbs-up. Super subtle, girls. Thanks. (Luckily, Dave didn't notice them. I don't think.)

"For what it's worth," he adds, "I think you should do it. And if you want some pointers, I can show you around."

I nod. At least, I think I nod. My head has kind of gone numb.

"How about later this week, maybe the day before the competition?" he asks. "I know I need to get in all the practice that I can manage—it'll be my first time in the intermediate category."

My inner monologue is shrieking and wondering why I didn't think to ask him if he was competing (smooth move, Lindsay), and my sensors are going off and telling me that a superhero would never be this tongue-tied—we're always ready with a witty quip—but all I can do is stammer out, "Sure, that sounds g-good."

He smiles and nods, but then his friend, dressed in all black and covered with logos of bike brands, rolls over and glares at me. Not to be judgmental but . . . I don't like his face or his attitude. He's got dirty-blond hair sticking out of the top of his helmet, and while he might pass as cute if he were looking friendly and smiling, his closed-off face makes him seem like he just doesn't want to be friends with anyone. And he doesn't look nearly as cool as Phoebe does when she's wearing all black.

"Are you ready to go actually ride bikes now?" he asks Dave, ignoring me as he stands right between us.

"I was talking to Lindsay," Dave says, quickly shooting me a smile. I try to smile back at him, but before my lips curl up, the kid is talking again and my smile immediately stops.

"Why? Girls shouldn't even be here," the scrawny kid replies, still not actually acknowledging me, just staring accusingly at Dave like he's the one in the wrong here. "She's probably with that loser tomboy Ali and that stupid princess Jen. They just get in the way every time I'm trying to practice, and with the competition coming up, it's so annoying. I mean, they're not going to win that gold frame, but I absolutely can . . . if they'd stop getting in the way."

It's so rude and out of nowhere that I can't even think of a retort.

"Ignore him," Dave says, looking over jerk boy's shoulder at me. "He's just in a bad mood today. Sam, why don't you go over to the expert line and get started working on those jumps. You need all the practice you can get if you really think you stand a chance of winning that bike frame." He doesn't say that in a mean way, just dismissive, so Sam doesn't really have a choice but to leave us alone.

As Sam rolls away muttering about girls getting in the way, Dave apologizes for him. "He's always been kind of mean," he explains. "I never liked hanging out with him

when we were kids, and since he started competing on the bike, he's been even harder to deal with—especially with the competition coming up and that gold frame as a prize. He's a total show-off, but he's also not that good compared to some of the guys who ride here, so he takes it out on the new kids in the park."

"Are there other guys like him here too?" I ask—and I'm afraid that if the answer is yes, I'm going to just go wait in the van and never come back.

Dave smiles. "Luckily, not too many. Sam's having a tough time right now especially because his older sister has been doing really well in competitions out on the West Coast, and he hates getting shown up by her. I think that's why he's especially annoyed to see you girls coming in more often."

"So why do you hang out with him?" I ask. "He seems to know you pretty well."

"Yeah, his parents and mine are good friends, so we carpool here," Dave explains, looking pained. "I'm kind of stuck with him, especially when his other friends aren't around."

"He has other friends?" I'm surprised that I managed to come up with something that good. Also, Dave is pretty thoughtful for a boy. Most of the boys I know at school are . . . well, they're low-level henchmen at best. But Dave seems like he has hero potential.

Dave gets a huge grin on his face and laughs. "Well,

he has other guys who stand around and talk about how great they are at riding bikes," he says. "But with friends like those . . ."

"Who needs enemies," we finish in unison, and laugh.

"I hope Sam being a jerk doesn't mean you think I'm a jerk too," Dave says suddenly.

"I think you're okay. Just jerk-adjacent," I say, smiling.

"Cool. I should go over there," he says, gesturing toward the jump line. "So, see you soon?"

"You got it."

≋ Training Log ≋

No time for writing, and even if I had time, I would be extremely nervous that someday my mother would stumble onto this log and (a) see a whole lot of curse words about what a jerk (that wasn't a curse word, I'm just being polite) Sam is, and (b) see me doodle some hearts around Dave's name. Yeah, I've turned into a total cliché, straight out of a cheesy movie.

> Le sigh,
> Lindsay
> (Good flow, but it's missing a certain something.)

CHAPTER 21

"So I hear Dave is going to work with you on your jumps," Phoebe says as soon as I slide into the van next to her. How does she do that?

"How do you know that?" I ask. Is there some kind of secret video room she's watching from? Or does she have me bugged?

"I have my ways," she says cryptically. "But that's not the point. How do you feel about it?"

"Like I could throw up," I say honestly. "In a good way, though . . . I think. What if I fall in front of him?"

"He'll think you're cooler if you do," Phoebe replies.

I just stare at her, because that makes absolutely no sense.

"It's not about being great at riding the jumps," she says. "It's that you're willing to try them. Being confident means doing stuff that scares you, and being willing to try and fail. Say you go in tomorrow and you just focus on not falling. Sure, you might not fall in front of Dave, but you also won't get any better, and you won't impress him, or yourself. You don't want to take dangerous risks, but you do have to be willing to feel a little silly—or get a couple of bruises—if you want to improve. If you're not afraid of crashing, you're much more likely to nail a trick. . . . But if you don't even make an attempt, you're never going to jump higher."

Huh.

"Also, that guy Sam is a jerk, just so you know," Phoebe says. "Between you and me, I don't think Sam is even that bad, really. He's just really insecure, and he takes it out on people in a way that stinks. But that cute guy, Dave, who you were talking to—he's one of the good guys. And trust me, he won't be laughing at you if you crash. He'll think it's cool that you're trying new things."

"Yeah, I just don't like bullies, and I know for sure Dave isn't one," I say . . . but I admit, while Dave was cool to me, it makes me a little nervous knowing that he spends time with someone as mean as Sam.

"No, he's not," Phoebe says. "Trust me, I have my sources." She seems secretive, so I let it go.

"Hey, can I ask you one more thing?"

"Of course. What's up?"

"Why are you trying so hard to make sure I have friends?"

Phoebe looks over at me. "Linds, you probably don't remember what I was like when I was your age, but knowing me now, after all these talks that we've had, do you really believe that I was ever a super-popular kid at school?"

I picture Phoebe when I was just a little kid and she'd come over for family dinners, strutting in wearing all black and sitting in the corner with a book and her headphones on. She looked scary but cool. All attitude and confidence.

"You just seemed really confident, so I bet you had a ton of friends," I say, and Phoebe looks sad.

"Linds, I wasn't confident at all! I was just super shy—that's why I was reading a book all the time, even when I was at your house. I didn't know how to talk to people, so I just read and listened to music. I was the exact same way at school—and trust me, the girl wearing weird clothes wasn't exactly sitting at the cool table. And sure, reading is awesome, but now that I have friends and ride bikes and play music with the Chainbreakers, I realize how much I missed," she says. "And I don't want that for you. It sucks."

I never really thought of being alone as being a bad thing, but since I've started hanging out with Jen and Ali, and since Dave has been talking to me (not much, but still!), I've been having more fun than I expected. While it hasn't been that long, I feel like Jen and Ali and I could really become great friends—especially now that I know Jen and I have more in common than I thought. I wonder if I'll stay friends with them during the school year, and if I should maybe start making more friends in school. I'm not going to throw away my comic books, but it would be nice to have some people to talk to about them—and bikes!—every once in a while.

"Hey, Phoebe—one more thing. Why did you start

riding?" I ask. I can't believe I haven't thought of it before. "And why doesn't your mom like that you ride?"

"What makes you say that she doesn't like it?" Phoebe asks, and I blush.

"I maybe heard her on the phone with my mom talking about you training with your dad, and your mom complaining that she was really scared that you were training together. I sort of thought she meant supervillain training, but now that I know about the bikes, I figure she means that Tío Carlos rides with you."

"You're not wrong," Phoebe sighs. "Well, except about the supervillain part anyway. So you probably don't know, but my dad used to be a pro bike racer in Mexico back in the eighties. He was pretty good, but not really well known or anything. He raced for a couple of years, but he had a bad crash, and while he was recovering, they moved to the US. By the time he had recovered, he already had a teaching job, and since Mom was so worried about him, he stopped racing totally. And they don't talk about it much because it was so long ago, but Dad still rides a bunch for fun. He talked me into going out on a few rides with him a couple of years ago, and I got hooked."

Wow. My uncle was a professional bike racer? That is *so* cool!

"Wait, he rides BMX bikes?" I ask.

Phoebe laughs. "No way. He calls those toy bikes. He was a road cyclist; he rode one of those bikes with the skinny tires—like that one." As we pull into the garage, she points at the bike that I never see her ride that's sitting in the corner. It's white and blue, unlike the rest of her bikes, which are black with flames. "He got that one for me, but it's not my favorite."

Clearly. It looks a little dusty.

"We still ride together a lot, though," she adds. "We just don't always agree on the most fun way to ride. I tried out the BMX bike once on a snowy day a few winters ago and got hooked."

"I guess that's like Mom and I both liking to read, but her not liking comic books," I say.

"Exactly."

We grin at each other, totally on the same page.

"And that's why your mom is so worried about you," I say, slowly putting the puzzle together. "And you were training to be a cyclist, not to take over the world."

"You still kinda sorta think I might be a supervillain, don't you?" Phoebe asks, but she's laughing as she says it.

"Wellll . . . maybe a teeny bit," I admit.

"I can live with that," she says, looking satisfied. "So, go out there and maybe crash your bike."

I laugh, even though I know she's a teensy bit serious.

Training Log

I opened my eyes and for a second had no idea where I was. Then I remembered I was at Phoebe's, and it was her voice I heard coming from the other room, ranting on the phone.

"I can't believe it!" she was shouting, and that's what caught my attention.

This is weird. Normally, she's quieter in the morning. In fact, that's kind of a rule of hers. She says that real bike racers "ease their way into their mornings." That means having some quiet time to let your mind and body wake up, before jumping on the bike and getting started with the day. She doesn't play loud music, watch TV, or even practice riding until she's done her meditation and had some breakfast, and since I got here, I've started trying to do the same thing. Normally, I'd be meditating in here, but she's yelling so much right now that it's sort of hard to get my zen on, so I figured I'd write instead. Or do some detective work—back to superhero basics!

Superhero Tip: The powers of observation only count as eavesdropping if the person you're listening to isn't screaming at top volume.

This bears investigating,
Lindsay
(At least that's somewhat heroic.)

CHAPTER 22

I walk out to the kitchen and sit at the counter so she knows I'm awake, and she nods in my direction to acknowledge me before scowling at the phone. (I think the nod meant, "Good morning. Make your own breakfast because I am ANGRY.")

"I don't understand. What do you mean, there's no girls' categories?" she's saying. "Why don't the girls get their own categories? What makes them think there aren't any girls who would want to compete?"

She looks at me, and I start to get a sinking feeling in my stomach. Before I can shake my head at her, she's

barreling on. "My cousin Lindsay and her two friends want to compete, and they're going to!"

I'm shaking my head so hard that I very nearly fall off the stool. I'm sure I'm shouting "NO!" at the top of my lungs, but she doesn't seem to hear me, so I must just be screaming in my mind. But still—competing with girls was scary enough, and now she wants to showcase us competing against the boys?

Is she crazy? She is a supervillain. I knew it!

In fact, she really looks like one now. She's grinning at me and looking just a little scary—exactly like I imagined her looking as a supervillain who just got the upper hand.

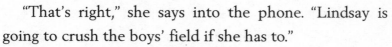

"That's right," she says into the phone. "Lindsay is going to crush the boys' field if she has to."

She clearly doesn't like the answer she gets on the other end of the phone.

"Fine! We'll see you there," she says dramatically before hanging up.

She puts out a hand and pulls me to standing.

"So," she says, smiling like nothing has happened and she hasn't just committed me to something even more insane than I already thought it was. She sips her coffee slowly, and I know I'm right to feel nervous. She's scary when she's angry. "It seems as though they decided not to have categories for the girls and women who wanted to do this jump competition. But that's just fine. You three will show those stuffy old guys that you don't just deserve your own category; you need one so that the guys have a chance to win too!"

I have goose bumps, and I'm not sure if they're good or bad.

"So what does this all mean, exactly?" I ask.

"It means your field just got a lot bigger, but you're going to be great," she says, sipping again. The steam from her coffee wafts around her face, and it looks just a bit more villainous than usual.

"No, no, no," I say, but she steamrolls over me.

"You'd better get changed. We have some training to do if you three are going to crush in the competition. Call Ali and Jen."

I'm really afraid they're going to love this plan, and I have to admit, something about how excited and angry Phoebe was about there being no girls' competition has me a little excited too. More terrified than excited, for sure, but competing against the boys? Competition in general? The more I think about it, the sicker I feel.

But at the same time, there's a little spark in my stomach, something that seems like it's saying, "This could be really cool." I mean, it is super unfair—and maybe we can help prove a point.

After all, heroes are only made when faced with hardship and strife, right?

Right?!

≋ Training Log ≋

As we drive to the gym, Phoebe takes another call from Joyride's owner, Matt. He's as upset with the promoter of the competition as Phoebe, but he says he can't do anything, since he already signed contracts with the companies that are sponsoring the competition. Still, from what I can hear—and Phoebe isn't exactly being quiet—Matt is totally on board with us competing, and he's offered whatever help he can give.

That means Phoebe is asking for keys to the park so we can come early and stay late to practice, which sounds okay to me, as long as I can still get some reading done during the day. Granted, my reading has been swapped out, since on our way to the car, Phoebe handed me a stack of training manuals and BMX magazines "for research," but this feels like a school project I'm excited about, not just a ton of extra work. (The general theme of BMX magazines seems to be big fonts, bright colors, and really crazy stunts that I don't think I could ever land in a million years, but they are fun to flip through!)

And yeah, sometimes I like school projects. Sue me.

Superhero Tip: I just read about this cool idea of "flow state" that riders get into when doing really intense tricks or jumps. It's like when you're concentrating so hard that, suddenly, you're not really concentrating, just in this state of being awesome and totally into what you're doing. I'm not sure how to get to that point but the key seems to be "practice a lot."

Forever nerdy,
Lindsay
(Still accurate, I'm afraid.)

CHAPTER 23

Lucky for Ali and Jen, they're ready and waiting when we get there; otherwise, the wrath of Phoebe might have been a bit too much for any one person to handle—she seems mad enough to break bones, or bike frames.

She slams the door to the van and stalks toward the Joyride entrance—which would have looked terrifying if the car alarm hadn't started beeping and she hadn't forgotten her bike. Once she turns off the alarm and grabs her bike, her stalking slows considerably and her shoulders are a bit more hunched. But she still looks angry as she walks in. As soon as Matt spots her, he throws up his hands like he's protesting his innocence. Which I suppose he is.

Phoebe huddles with Ali, Jen, and me in a corner, pointedly not speaking to Matt (presumably because, as a guy, he counts as the enemy right now), and fills them in on what's happening with the competition.

"I know it might seem scarier to be up against the guys and in the mix with them, but it's even more important that you all compete," she tells us, looking very, very serious. "I can't believe we're not getting a category for you girls, but we're still going to rock it."

She brightens up a bit and grins widely at us. "I know

you can absolutely, positively, crush the competition, guys or girls or both. So are you in?"

Jen perks up immediately. "I've never raced against boys before," she says. "Women always have their own categories in bike races—it's not fair otherwise!"

"I know," says Phoebe. "It's not fair to you girls. But I know what some of the guys in your category are riding like, and I know you'll do just fine competing against them. And it's important that we show the event sponsors that women are here and want to ride. You girls are paving the way for lots more girls."

To be honest, knowing that the competition matters to Phoebe so much kind of makes me even more nervous—and excited. I figured it would be us, and maybe a couple of other girls our age, but now that I know we're competing against some really good, really serious guys, it's more intimidating. But at the same time, knowing that it is unfair that the girls don't get their own race makes me angry, and that gets me pretty pumped up. It makes the competition matter more, knowing the stakes aren't just "how well I finish"—us competing, like Phoebe says, might mean that next time, we do get our own category and get to show that girls are here, and want to stake our claim in biking.

So I nod, maybe twitching a little as I do it, but of course I'm in.

I'm not the only one who has a lot more nervous

energy pumping. Of course, at the word "contest," and after being told we aren't supposed to be able to compete, Jen's eyes lit up.

"I'm absolutely in," she announces, despite not yet actually being able to get any air over the jumps in the small jump line—at least, not without crashing or stalling out. But I think she really, really wants to start being competitive again, and Phoebe's anger seems to stoke that fire.

"Actually," she says, "I think I might like not competing just against other girls—I kind of want to see where I stack up against the guys."

"It does kind of take some pressure off in a weird way, doesn't it?" I say. I've been thinking about this furiously: if we compete against the guys as well, it's less about us against each other and more of a united girl-power front. That's easier for me to get behind.

Ali doesn't perk up as quickly. "I just don't think I'll be that good," she admits. But Phoebe explains that it's not about racing fast or hitting the biggest jumps in the park.

"For your category, you'll be jumping on the same line we've been practicing on this whole time. It's about showcasing your jumps and tricks against a bunch of other beginners—they just happen to be guys," she says.

At that, Ali seems a little less nervous, and she bursts out with a huge smile.

"My brothers are going to freak!" she crows. She mentioned the other night that she has three older brothers—

all racers—and I'm realizing just how hard she tries to measure up to them. This might be her chance. With how happy she and Jen look, it's hard for me to keep feeling like entering this competition is a huge mistake. It might actually be fun.

My feelings are all over the place. One minute, I'm ready to compete and I want to win; the next minute, I'm wondering if my bike and I could fit under Phoebe's desk in her office and I can just stay there for the day. Or call Tía Maria to take me with her so I can skip being around bikes altogether. But mostly, the excitement is starting to win out.

Phoebe triumphantly stalks behind the desk to let Matt know that we're all okay with the category change. After she does that—poor Matt, I can see he's smiling at her and nodding but she's still glaring—she motions us over to the pump track.

"I thought we did this already," Jen complains.

"That's what I was saying to you guys before," Phoebe says, only slightly impatiently. "It's not about kind of nailing a move and moving on to something huge; it's about doing the little stuff over and over until you can do it in your sleep."

"But I can do it in my sleep. This is boring!" Jen whines. "What about the bigger pump track? When do we get on that?"

"Get around the track right now without a single pedal

stroke and we'll move on," say Phoebe, unmoved by Jen's pleas.

Jen swaggers over to the line, pulling her pink helmet off her bike's handlebars and slipping it over her perfect braid carefully. "No problem," she says, flicking her hair and looking confident—she's got swagger, I'll give her that.

She starts onto the loop by taking a few big pedal strokes so she drops in with good speed, but she has six bumps to roll over without any more pedaling allowed. One hump, and she's over. Two, she makes it. When she clears the third, I'm starting to doubt whether Phoebe was right, but on the fourth, she wavers a bit, almost not making it down the other side. She rolls into the fifth bump . . . and rolls almost immediately backward and off the track, not having gained enough speed to go up and over.

For a second, Jen looks like she really wants to throw her bike—we know she's done it before—but she pulls back a bit, smiles, and waves at us instead. She rolls back over to the starting ledge and just asks how she can get faster. Phoebe smiles and goes back to her explanation of how to use your body to pull up and push over to maximize speed on each bump of the track.

"Trust me," she says. "When the bumps are ten feet high instead of two, you're going to really, really want to make it over them every time. It's one thing to roll backward or clip a pedal here—when you fall, it's not a big deal. But when you're on the big jumps, it's going to hurt a lot more." She gestures over to the room with the expert lines, where guys are hurtling through the air. "Those guys? They all practice here before they go out there, even if they've been riding for years. So let's get started. Ten laps, everybody!"

Ali is the first to roll out, and I follow. Jen stays behind a minute and whispers something to Phoebe, and Phoebe squeezes her shoulder in response.

After what feels like five hundred trips around the small oval—I know it's only ten, but it seems like so much more—my arms are getting sore. We take a water break, and while I'm digging in my backpack for my bottle, Dave rolls up and skids to a dramatic stop in front of me. He's looking skater-boy cool in a flannel and skinny jeans, and a helmet covered in stickers.

But this time, I'm not nearly as intimidated as when I first bumped into him. Thanks to my shopping spree, I have on black leggings and a deep purple long-sleeved tunic top. It's nothing fancy, but with my hair braided and a plain black helmet on, I think I look kind of like Catwoman on her day off.

"You were looking smooth on the pump track," he says with a smile.

He saw me riding?! Since I'm messing around with my backpack, it's easier to talk without looking directly at him. "Thanks," I say. (Good start.) "Are you practicing anything cool?" (Yes! Full sentence!)

He launches into a description of one of the bigger jump lines. Even hearing him talking about it sounds terrifying, but without thinking, I blurt out that we all are still competing, even though there isn't a girls' category.

"That's so rad!" he says enthusiastically. "And you're going to do great."

"Thanks, but I'm not sure it's going to go so well," I say. It's so easy to be excited about it when Phoebe is giving us a motivational speech, but when I'm in my own head, it gets nerve-racking.

"Don't worry about it. You're not going to be doing the big lines unless you want to. Phoebe probably entered you in the beginner category. Right, Phoebe?" he shouts the last part as Phoebe happens to scoot by. She skids to the same super-cool stop as Dave and gives him a half hug, half shoulder squeeze.

"What are you guys talking about?" she asks innocently, but I know by her expression that she's going to be interrogating me later.

We actually end up interrogating each other in the van as we're leaving. (We would make an excellent dynamic duo fighting crime together. If we don't end up talking over each other and completely ignoring the bad guy we're trying to question.)

"What was it that Jen whispered to you before we

started practicing again?" I ask, curiosity getting the better of me.

"She apologized," Phoebe says happily, and I'm pretty surprised.

"For what?" I ask.

"She's been having a hard time ever since her parents made her stop racing. . . . Apparently, she wasn't having an easy time in school and she was pretty unhappy while she was racing—and really, really unhappy when she didn't win. But that's her story to tell."

"No one likes to lose," I point out. "And she told us that already."

"Of course," Phoebe says. "But there's a difference between being bummed about losing for a few minutes and letting it control your life. A lot of kids get like that. They get into riding bikes, start racing a bit and having some good results, and completely forget about what makes riding fun. Competition is great, but it's not the only thing there is to riding."

"Then why do you care so much that there isn't a spot for girls to compete in a couple of weeks?"

"That's not about racing, exactly," Phoebe hedges. "That's about fairness and getting more girls into riding bikes in general. Like I said, a lot of kids are like Jen and really want to compete in something. Sports as a kid should be about fun. Do you remember that time your mom put you in soccer?"

"I hated it," I say passionately. "I remember I cried before every practice."

"Yeah, but you were stuck because your mom thought you needed to play a team sport to have fun outside. But I bet you were happier just running around outside pretending to be Batman and doing your own thing."

She makes an excellent point. "That's true," I say.

"But a ton of those kids had a lot of fun on your soccer team," she points out. "And the nice thing with these jump competitions is that it's sort of the best of both worlds. It's a competition, but at the end of the day, we all just want to hang out and ride bikes," she says, before pausing and adding, "And, of course, it's pretty sweet when you do win."

Training Log

Normally, this would be the point in a movie where a training montage happens. In reality, though, Phoebe has just been working us super hard at the park for the last ten days, and frankly, I haven't had the time or energy to update my training log. Sorry!

I've since graduated from the kiddie line, done what feels like thousands of loops around the park, crashed so many times that, despite wearing pads, my knees and elbows feel permanently bruised, and cried at least once a day. I've been coming home completely exhausted, sore, and ready to fall into bed, but it doesn't stop there.

Phoebe is a woman possessed. She's made me start eating tons of healthier foods—even our pizzas are now covered with so many veggies that I can't see the cheese, and it's whole-grain crust instead of white. Yesterday and the day before, she made me drink a protein shake after we finished training. And at night, instead of watching cartoons, we've been watching BMX videos.

And I kind of like it.

But if she asks, I'd never admit it. (I think she knows anyway.)

Superhero Tip: You are what you eat. And I miss being Doritos.

Getting tougher by the day,
Lindsay
(Not bad!)

CHAPTER 24

It's early, as usual, since we have yet another practice to get to. I'm sitting at the table eating my yogurt and berries—another Phoebe mandate in her attempt to keep us all healthy and competition-ready. When we were at the park the other day, she handed all three of us a list with good foods we should be eating (vegetables, mostly), plus a bunch of notes about when we should be going to bed at night (early) and how many planks we should be doing every morning as our strength training (a lot). Lucky for Jen and Ali, they don't live with her watching them like a hawk every day, pushing spinach-chicken rice bowls for every other meal and timing how long they can hold a plank. (I'm up to fifteen seconds.)

It's exhausting—I thought being a bike rider meant just, you know, riding a bike, but I'm starting to see there's a lot more to it than that.

While I'm trying to get through the last few bites of berries, Phoebe slides her phone over to me. "Hit play," she says.

I press play. Loud rock music blares through the phone speakers. I bop along to the song, completely immersed.

"I used my band's song," she admits. It's pretty catchy, I have to say. She's never actually played any of her stuff for me before, but there's a good beat, and I can hear her growly voice—the one I usually only hear before she's had coffee in the morning—coming through.

"You guys sound awesome!" I say, but I'm more interested in the video she's taken of Jen, Ali, and me. It shows us on our first day falling down and doing planks, then gradually getting smoother on the pump track. I see the time I refused to go down the jump line. It even shows me chatting with Dave a couple of times, at first looking super terrified but, by the end of the video, rolling past him and high-fiving as we ride in different directions.

As the music hits the chorus for the second time, I can really see the progress that we made once we started working on the jump lines. (Jump lines are straight lines of bumps similar to the ones on the pump track, but higher. The idea is to get some air as you go over them.) The pump track is like a warm-up loop for us now, even though even a few sessions ago, it seemed like it was the hardest thing in the world to get through.

And sure, we're not soaring through the air, and I'm not doing backflips into a foam pit, but all three of us are getting a little bit of daylight under our wheels as we go up and over the jumps, and I can definitely tell that I've gotten a lot smoother just in the last week.

It hasn't been that long, but the montage really shows me just how much has changed since Phoebe came into my life. Even my clothes in the first couple of clips are so different—I can't believe what a change just dressing more "my style" has made for me! How did she know those videos from our first few sessions would come in handy? She must be kind of psychic.

Before I really think about it, I slide off my stool and run around to give her a hug. "I'm pretty proud of you, you know?" she says.

I nod.

"So . . . now you're ready to go practice again?" she asks, and I roll my eyes as I head off to get changed. But there's definitely a bit more spring in my step than I would have had before, and that song is totally stuck in my head.

Once I'm dressed and packed, I wander into Phoebe's bedroom to check if she's ready to go. While I wait for her to finish typing an email, I glance around. I've never really noticed how she decorated in here before.

"Who's that?" I ask, pointing at a picture on the wall, totally curious—and, I admit, trying to stall so we don't have to go to practice quite yet. I'm excited but also a little nervous every time we go. Above Phoebe's desk, she has a poster of a girl ripping over a track on a BMX bike, well ahead of the competition. A smaller poster next to it shows the same girl standing proudly on a podium, holding an Olympic gold medal. I didn't even know BMX was in the Olympics!

"That's Mariana Pajón Londoño, a Colombian BMXer," Phoebe says.

"I didn't realize there were any Latin American bike racers," I admit. "I never heard of her."

"She won two medals in the Rio Summer Olympics, and she's known as the Queen of BMX," Phoebe tells me. "I like having that poster up to remind me that there are Latin American female racers out there—and we're adding more all the time," she adds, nudging me.

I grin. "I'm going to read more about her," I say.

"Of course you are," Phoebe laughs. "Now, about that practice session . . ."

Right. We don't just talk about cool riders, we are the cool riders! We pile into the van and head to Joyride.

When we get there, Ali and Jen are already eagerly waiting for us, helmets on, rolling around in the warm-up area. I think they just wanted to skip having to do planks again and they're hoping having helmets already on will prevent Phoebe from torturing us. I know better.

I'm right, and of course, we start with planks. "You girls are going to thank me for this later," Phoebe says cheerfully as she has us drop into that dreaded push-up position and hold it.

I don't believe her.

Once we're finally finished warming up, Phoebe tells us that today, we're going to finally try out the jump line where the competition will be. It's not that different from the pump track we've done most of our practicing on, but the long line of rollers goes straight, only banking at the far wall of the park. It ends there, and you ride down the flat lane on the side of it to start all over again. Every time I roll past it while we're here, there are a few kids going over the jumps, smoothly flying into the air at the top and casually landing on the backside. And because there are five lanes, all with different height rollers, ranging from five feet all the way to fifteen feet high, there are usually enough people riding at once to make you dizzy just watching.

In a word, it's terrifying. But it's also going to be where we'll need to ride in the competition. Phoebe leads us over to the platform where the drop-in for the lowest jump line is. For a minute, we just stand there, all staring at it.

"That's not so scary," Jen says. But I can see she's gripping her bars a little bit tighter than normal.

Ali looks less scared. "These are like what we have in our backyard," she admits, sounding relieved. "This is the highest we'll have to do?"

Phoebe nods. "The height and rolling over them shouldn't be a problem for any of you," she says. "But we want to focus on getting your technique good enough that you're actually getting a little bit of air and really pumping over each roller. Remember on the pump track, when each of you has almost fallen off because you've run out of speed? If that happens here, you'll be okay, but you won't make it too far in the competition."

"I'll go first," Ali volunteers, pushing her bike to the top of the drop-in.

"Go for it," Phoebe says, and Ali pushes off and down the steep ramp. She pedals a couple of times, and then she's going up the first of the rollers. She clears it but doesn't get up in the air at all.

"Push your arms down!" Phoebe shouts as Ali descends the back of the roller and heads toward the second. On the second one, she's a little slower going up, but at the top she listens to Phoebe's instructions and pushes her arms a bit forward and down on the bars, urging her weight toward the front of the bike.

"See how that helped her gather speed?" Phoebe asks us as we see Ali ride up the third roller more quickly.

"I can do that," Jen says, looking a bit more confident. I nod as well—it's not that different from the pump track, really.

Ali almost loses momentum on the last roller but pedals once between her descent and the little climb and saves it. She turns around and rolls back to us, a bit more flushed and sweaty than when she started. "That was a good save," Phoebe tells her. "But you'll lose points for that in competition, so let's keep working on that. And to get a bit more pop—maybe even some air—at the top of the rollers, you need to pull up on the bars and get weightless right at the top, and then immediately push down on the front end of the bike, like you've been doing.

It sounds a little confusing, I know, but think of it like you're trying to hop over the top of the roller instead of rolling over it or bouncing on top of it."

"Pretend the middle of the roller is cut out, like a Batman-versus-Joker death trap," I interject, and Phoebe laughs.

"Just like that," she agrees.

I try it out, and it's a lot harder than it looks. I don't fall, though, and only pedal twice on my first try. Jen, surprisingly, struggles more than either of us. "Road racers don't use their arms," she informs us when we're all back on the platform.

"That's kind of true," says Phoebe. "But we're not on the road bike now. That's why we've been doing things like planks, though, so your arms and core are strong enough for tricks like this."

She demonstrates and makes getting into the air on each roller—and not pedaling through the jump line—look super easy. But she is sweaty when she rolls back to us, so it can't be that easy for her.

By the time practice is officially over for the day, my arms are feeling exhausted. Phoebe calls that "pump," where all the blood and lactic acid (whatever that is) pools in your arms and makes the muscles feel tired. But the three of us have managed to get through the line without any pedal strokes, and we're even starting to make a little progress getting into the air.

Plus, Jen snuck in brownies that her grandma made for her, so I got to actually have some junk food. I've never liked her more!

On the last run of our session, I finally got my wheels off the ground, just a tiny bit. I felt the same way I did the first day Phoebe had me "flying" into the foam pit . . . except this is so much better. I earned it this time.

It's a pretty cool feeling. Even if it left me so tired that as soon as we get in the van to go home, I fall asleep.

⇒ Training Log ⇐

I'm still nervous about the competition, but honestly, having friends over for dinner and not freaking out about it is probably even crazier than the fact that I'm going to be competing on a bike. In front of judges! Speaking of dinner, Jen and Ali are on their way over for our now semi-regular end-of-week dinner at the apartment, and we've cooked up some pretty great-smelling curry with a ton of veggies—we don't just eat pizza and Mexican food! Penguin is even begging at the table, and I had no idea dogs liked vegetables. Doorbell is ringing, so I should probably stop writing and answer it. I'm not even dreading it.

Superhero Tip: The more vegetables you eat, the better they start tasting. And you do start feeling healthier and more superhero-like. It's annoying when parents are right when they say spinach is A Good Thing.

Ending on a hungry note,
Lindsay
(Why do I write so much about food?)

CHAPTER 25

We're clustered around the table finishing the last bites of utterly delicious curry, when Phoebe tells us that training for the day isn't quite over yet. But as the three of us get up and start heading for our bikes, she calls us back to the table.

"We've done a ton of great work on the bikes this week," she says. "But now we need to do a little bit of off-bike training as well."

"What, more planks?" Jen asks. (We were all thinking it . . . and dreading it.)

"No," Phoebe replies. "I'm talking about visualization. It's really helpful, especially when you're getting ready for a competition like this one and you're feeling nervous."

"How do you do it?" Ali asks eagerly.

"What are you scared of?" Jen asks. "You're better than we are!"

"I'm afraid I'll mess something up and my brothers will see," she says. "Even though they're not going to be there, I'm afraid someone will get me on video epically messing up a jump, and it'll get back to them."

"Visualization is just what you need, then," Phoebe says. She explains that visualization is just a simple focusing exercise that's like daydreaming. "You're imagining the day of the competition, and everything leading up to your start, then running through the perfect jump line. You're seeing yourself taking each jump smoothly, hitting the top of the whoop and getting a little air, coming down the backside without pedaling, and using your momentum to hit the next," she adds.

She has us close our eyes and envision ourselves nailing each series of jumps. I'm having trouble trying to make a mental image, though. And then I think about my journal and almost instantly, my brain snaps to attention and I'm writing the scene. "I'm effortlessly floating over each jump, almost weightless. My bike hovers underneath me, and I can feel my feet firm on the pedals while my hands gently grip the handlebars. My heart is beating faster, but I feel calm. My eyes are open, and when I hit the second jump, I fly up and over, with so much air that I have time to flick my bike out to my right side and bring it back to center before I touch back down."

Once we've all done that for a couple of minutes, Phoebe tells us to open our eyes. "Good job," Phoebe says, "but one time isn't enough. You'll need to do this every day before the competition."

"Can I write about it?" I ask.

"What do you mean?"

I explain that I usually write out my daydreams into stories, which Phoebe says is a great idea. "Whatever will get that picture in your head and keep it there until you need it on the big day," she says.

"What about making a collage of cool girls jumping?" asks Jen, and Phoebe answers that that's also a great idea, as long as she's not just imagining those girls doing cool tricks.

"It only works if you can see yourself doing these tricks and jumps, not picturing other people doing them," she adds.

"That makes sense," Jen says. "I'm just having a hard time seeing myself jumping. I keep thinking about the last road race that I did—and didn't win." She looks pretty bummed out, like just talking about it is bringing up those bad memories.

"But now that it's been a while, was losing really so bad?" I ask, a little nervously. I don't want her to get mad at me, but I'm curious. "I mean, you came here and met us, and now you're doing something that's also pretty cool."

"I guess that's true," Jen says, smiling a teensy bit. "It's been pretty fun."

Ali looks glum. "I keep picturing myself falling and my brothers rolling by. Or hopping over me," she says sadly.

"Just relax," Phoebe advises. "Maybe start imagining yourself on a smaller jump line, with no one watching. I know it's hard to stop worrying about what they think of you. If you let them get in your head, you'll probably tense up more when you're in the middle of the competition."

After a few more minutes of practice, with Phoebe guiding us with our eyes closed as she describes a perfect jump line set, I think I'm really getting the hang of it. Ali looks a lot cheerier too. "I think I'm doing it right now," she says. "That time, I managed to get around my brother!"

"Next, try hopping over him," Phoebe adds, and we all giggle.

Training Log

Training is hard. And everything hurts.

I might not make it,
Lindsay
(Seriously.)

CHAPTER 26

I think I'm going to die. This is at least the millionth time today that I've gone through the same medium-height jump line. My hands hurt. My stomach is sore. My legs feel like jelly. Phoebe just looks at her phone and motions to me to go again. I want to yell at her, but I'm honestly afraid that if I stop rolling, I'll fall over.

Before we started, she taught me what she calls the ponytail trick. When I'm jumping, I'm supposed to go for the feeling of my ponytail going up in the air and have it come back down when I hit the backside of the jump. If I feel it, it means I managed to get enough momentum to get in the air. If I don't, then I probably didn't get off the ground.

"Stop after this round!" she shouts as I drop in, down the steepest of the jumps and into a series of three-foot-tall rolling mini hills, trying to jump over the top of them. After another round where I only hit the floor with my pedal once, I stop at the top next to Phoebe, panting.

"Today is the day we're going to get you in the air."

"How was that round, though?" I ask.

"See for yourself," she says. "This was your first try."

I watch a video of myself pedaling like mad, rolling over the top of each of the little hills, the pedal hitting

the top of each one loudly, almost echoing. "Yikes," I say. "I really thought I was getting over the top."

"Yeah, I know how that feels," she says sympathetically. "But look . . ."

She scrolls down her phone and hits play again. "This was your last round," she says, holding out the phone. I wish I could say I was leaping tall buildings in a single bound, but I wasn't that impressive. Still, I only pedaled a couple of times, used my weight to push and pull over the hills, and even got the teensiest bit of air at the tops. And the one time I hit my pedal, it wasn't nearly as loud.

"See what a little extra practice can do?" Phoebe says, somewhat more smugly than she needed to, in my opinion.

"And," she adds, lowering her voice, "you're welcome."

"For what?" I ask.

"Hi, Lindsay!" I hear from behind me, just as Phoebe turns away and suddenly becomes a lot more interested in her bike.

"Hey, Dave," I manage, still a little out of breath. Great. He would show up when I'm red and sweaty and—let's be real—not exactly doing anything impressive.

"That was really good," he says, casually riding up the little hill to the platform that I always have to walk. "I think you're ready for the competition."

"I can't believe it's tomorrow," I say, feeling only slightly paralyzed.

"And with that in mind, I'm going to go hit the jump line a few more times," Phoebe says, and rolls off, but not before she winks at me. I'm pretty sure Dave sees her do it, but he pretends not to.

Dave steps in as she pedals happily away. "I think I owe you a jump lesson, right?" he asks. I nod.

"So I probably won't explain it that well, but you're already really close. You're getting up and over, and I know you can do the bunny hop where you lift your front wheel and your rear wheel, right?"

"You've been watching me?" I ask, and he reddens. I didn't realize I could be that clever! Caught him in the act.

"Just a little," he admits. "There aren't many girls here, so when a cool one comes in, I notice."

He called me cool!

"Anyway," he continues, kind of awkwardly, "what you want to do is combine the two. So as you go up and over the whoop on the track, you're bringing your front wheel, then your rear wheel, up in the air. Then you push back down on the backside so you have that momentum to keep going."

When I look confused, he laughs. "It sounds more complicated than it is. Really, you just need a bit more speed and confidence."

We run through it a couple of times, and I finally start to get it a bit more once he tells me to follow him and mimic what he's doing. That helps, and when I can keep up and feel my wheels leave the ground, my heart skips a beat. He gives me a couple of pointers about relaxing my legs and keeping my knees loose—not rigid and bent, but not perfectly straight either—and letting my core do more of the lifting than my arms. His little pieces of advice really help, and half an hour flies by.

I'm feeling more and more confident that, even if I don't win the competition, I won't embarrass myself either. In fact, I'm feeling so confident that I even give him a bit of advice—I noticed that his rear wheel wasn't making it as high over the jump as his front wheel, and when I point it out, he's able to make a slight correction that let him get both wheels higher. Success!

After we finish a bunch of runs and we're both a little out of breath, we still talk for a few more minutes. It's mostly about the competition at first, but then Dave asks if I ever listen to Phoebe's band and starts singing one of their songs. He isn't great at singing or air guitaring, and I'm giggling too much to join in on the chorus. But I do a mean air drum solo to make up for it. I'm also super impressed that Phoebe's band is so well known!

But then our nice moment is interrupted by yelling. I look over and see Ali and Sam shouting at each other across the room. "Should we go stop them?" I ask.

Dave looks frustrated. "I think Ali can take him. . . . But yeah, she shouldn't be stuck with him," he says, and we pedal toward them.

As we get closer, I notice Ali standing in front of Sam in line at the intermediate jump line—she might technically be a beginner, but Phoebe cleared her to get some practice on the bigger jumps too. She's good. "Too bad you can't ride like your brothers," I overhear him saying. I'm angry beyond words, and Ali's face is crumpled up like she's about to cry.

"Dude," Dave says, hopping off his bike and walking toward Sam. "Not cool."

"What?" Sam says. "Will someone tell her to get out of this line? She doesn't know how to ride."

"I've seen her riding and she's great," Dave says, glaring directly at Sam. "And you need to back off, now."

"Are you gonna make me?" Sam taunts, leering at Dave. I can't believe they ever hang out. Or that I'm about to see a fight. I'm looking around nervously for Phoebe, and Ali's face has gone white.

"Yeah," says Dave, and steps closer to him, and Sam suddenly looks a little nervous, like he's realized he's outnumbered. I notice that Dave is a few inches taller than him.

"Whatever," he mutters, grabbing his bike and pedaling away. He's trying to look casual, but he's pedaling pretty quickly.

"Thanks." Ali sniffs, and I give her a nudge.

"He really is a jerk," says Dave, and pats her on the shoulder.

"And forget what I said before—you don't really count as jerk-adjacent," I tell him, and he grins.

Dave says a quick goodbye and that he'll see us before it's our turn to go in the jump competition. He seems to know to give us a bit of space, which I appreciate, and Ali and I ride around together to cool down. She's quiet too, and I know how much Sam's taunts hurt her feelings. He's the worst.

It's not the best way to end our last practice day before the competition, but I'm going to use my anger at Sam to push myself to go just a teensy bit higher on the jumps.

And Ali, Jen, and I all take a minute together as we're about to leave the park to gather around the gold bike frame in the glass case as a bit of a good-luck charm and visualization moment.

"Whoever wins it, I'm just glad we got to meet," says Jen. And coming from her, that means a lot.

Training Log

I'm awake. It's still dark out and I'm hiding in bed, my eyes wide open—I've been awake for what feels like hours already. It's the day of the competition. What was I thinking? How did I let Phoebe talk me into this? How am I going to get out of it? Forget butterflies— I have full-grown bats smashing around in my stomach. I'm going to throw up. I have the flu. I have the Plague. I have . . . anything that will get me out of this competition.

> **Superhero Tip:** It's hard to be super when your heart won't stop racing.

Getting cut off because I hear footsteps,
Lindsay
(Not always going to work.)

CHAPTER 27

"Hot chocolate!" Phoebe singsongs, pushing my door open. She's unnaturally cheery compared to her normal, coffee-guzzling self. How is she so calm? Can't she see I'm dying?

I groan a little, and horrible person that she is, she just pulls my covers down. I knew she was an evil supervillain.

"You can't make me go," I mutter as she opens the window shades. Still dark.

"I know I can't, but you're going to want to once you're up," she says.

"Why would I want to?" I say, catching the whine in my voice. "I'm just going to lose."

"Okay, that's not positive thinking," she says. "Remember what we talked about with visualization, and how negative thinking can lead to making more mistakes, while positive thinking makes the competition easier and actually fun?"

"Yeah, yeah," I say. It all sounded convincing at the time, but when I know I have to perform in front of judges in a few hours, it's harder to stay calm and positive.

"Try visualizing for a couple of minutes," she says. "And maybe drink this hot chocolate. Remember that no matter how it goes, you get to hang out all day with your friends, there's a pizza party, and my band is playing. Plus Dave is going to be there and I happen to know he thinks you're cute." She sets my mug down and saunters out of the room.

I hop up and chase after her because, frankly, she makes an argument that I can't ignore.

"Wait! What do I wear?"

Soon enough, we're in Phoebe's van heading to Joyride. I'm still nervous about the competition, but thanks to Phoebe, I at least look the part.

I'm wearing my new black skinny jeans and a white T-shirt with a black triangle print, and my hair is in a sophisticated French braid. (It's because Phoebe did it—when my mom does my hair, I look like a little kid.) But the coolest part is the little spiky earrings Phoebe let me borrow. I look like me, only a little more punk—a little more like Phoebe, actually.

I don't think I want to look just like Phoebe, though she is pretty cool. She's ready for the day too, in her usual leggings, long sleeveless white top, and Joyride hoodie, and beat-up Converse high-tops and white tube socks. She should look ridiculous—most people in the same outfit would look like dorks—but she just looks comfortable, like a fashion model doing a shoot for casual BMX clothing.

Sitting in the passenger seat, I practice deep breathing and close my eyes, picturing myself hitting each jump smoothly. In my mind, I'm not soaring through the air ten feet off the ground, just making it over each jump cleanly—like Phoebe said, visualization works best when it's realistic; otherwise it's just daydreaming.

My butterflies have somewhat settled down as we get closer to Joyride, and now I've moved on to visualizing how the competition and the whole day is going to go. Since Phoebe has helped organize these competitions at Joyride in the past, she knows what to expect and has been drilling it into us. We know what's coming.

I'm going to spend most of the day just waiting for my turn to come, and then they'll call my name and I'll go over the easy jump line first. If that goes well—if the judges think it goes well—I'll go on to the beginners' round two. That's the second jump line, with the bigger jumps. Since it's for beginners, the competition only gets to the second jump line, but we'll have two chances to go through the line, and whoever the judges think jumps the highest and smoothest wins the competition.

And the prize? For each group in the competition, there's that bike frame, painted an awesome sparkly gold. It's been sitting in a glass trophy case right in the Joyride doorway since the competition was announced, and most of the time Jen can't stop staring at it like she can get it out of the case with the power of her mind. I'll settle for not making a fool of myself, crashing, or ripping my pants.

When we pull in, it seems really quiet. Too quiet (is what I would say if I were narrating a comic book).

"Lindsay, come on," Phoebe says impatiently.

Just inside the doorway, we can see a large group standing around the glass case where one of the prize bike frames had been standing, to show everyone what they were competing for.

But the glass case is empty.

"What happened?" Phoebe asks, elbowing a couple of other employees out of the way.

"Someone stole the frame and the prize check," Matt wails, practically falling into Phoebe.

"It's going to be fine, Matt." She pats his back awkwardly. "Matt! Snap out of it!" she says sternly as he keeps babbling about it all being over and the contest being ruined. "It's not that big of a deal. You can write a new check and cancel that one."

"But why would someone take the bike frame? It's expensive, but we have other nice stuff here too," he moans.

Phoebe walks away from him and goes behind the front desk to start looking through the employee area and bike shop, probably hoping that someone just moved it. She looks upset too, but I guess she's trying not to let Matt see. "I know I locked the door last night," she mutters, and I remember that Phoebe, Dave, Sam, and I were the last four to leave.

I spot Jen and Ali walking into Joyride's main entrance, looking stunned as they stare at the glass display surrounded by employees. I motion to them to follow me. While Phoebe starts pacing around in the back, I pull them over into the corner.

"The trophy frame is gone," I explain, to catch them up.

"I noticed," Jen says dryly, but she's obviously pretty upset. After all, what kind of first-place-obsessed rider wouldn't want to win and then parade around on a gold bike as a prize?

"Who do you think took it?" Ali asks in a hushed voice. This is why I like Ali—she's thinking exactly like me, reacting like a superhero detective would.

"Well, Dave, Sam, Phoebe, and I were the last to leave yesterday, and Matt was the first one in this morning. I don't think Matt stole his own trophy, so that either means someone broke in—or it was one of us." Ali looks at Jen like she's considering the possibility.

Ali shakes her head and dismisses it, though. "It couldn't have been one of us. We know that much."

"What about Dave?" Jen says, twirling her hair. "He seems shady to me."

"That's just because he talks to Lindsay instead of you," Ali shoots back before I can retort.

Jen reluctantly glances over and gives me an up-and-down appraisal. "Well, Lindsay is cute, and let's face it, she's pretty good on the jump line. . . . But I totally let you have him," she adds. I don't think she believes that, exactly, but Jen will be Jen.

"Gee, thanks," I say kind of sarcastically, and Jen nicely smiles at me.

"That just leaves Sam, but did you see him take anything with him when he left?" she asks. I hadn't.

"Has he come in yet?" Ali asks. I shake my head.

"So what do we do?" Jen asks, and I realize they're both looking at me. I have a squad! Finally!

"Well, I bet they're going to stick to the competition schedule, trophy or not, so we should still focus on the competition for ourselves," I say slowly, trying to think of the best possible plan. "But, Jen, you warm up by the front door and watch for Sam. Ali, you stay by the lockers, and I'll roll around by the boys' room so we don't miss him." They both giggle at that, but I'm too busy forming a plan. "If you see him, don't confront him. Let's follow him. If he took the frame last night but didn't manage to take it out of the park, we might be able to find it here somewhere."

They're nodding like I'm making sense. Which I think I am. "If one of us sees him, we should whistle as loud as we can, and try to follow far behind him so he doesn't notice us. Then the other two will join in, and we'll try to keep at least one of us on him at all times while we're warming up. Don't forget, Phoebe will kill us if we ignore the actual competition to follow that doofus around, especially if he doesn't actually have the trophy."

"Sounds like a good plan," Ali says, and Jen nods in approval.

"Hands in, girls," I say. (I can't help myself—I've always wanted to start the hand pile!) I put my hand out flat in the middle of us. Ali stacks hers on top of mine, and Jen puts hers on top—of course she has to be in the top spot.

"On three," I say, but Jen cuts me off before I can continue.

"What are we called?" she asks, and I can tell she's getting into the whole girl-detective concept.

"Shred Girls!" Ali says impulsively. Of course.

"Perfect!" I say. "All right. Shred Girls on three," I say. I try not to show it, but I'm really excited. I've never gotten to do something like this before, unless you count the time I was very briefly on a soccer team. Which I don't, because when we put our hands in, it knocked me to the ground, and then someone stepped on my glasses, my right hand, and the hem of my shorts, ripping them up the side.

First grade was rough.

"One," Jen says.

From Ali: "Two."

"Three!" I finish.

"Shred Girls!" we all say, just loud enough that Phoebe glances over.

"Act casual," I hiss at them

in a whisper, and we grab our bikes and head to our places to start practicing. The competition might be on, but I'm not nervous about it anymore. I'm ready to take on the world. Even that middle jump line.

"I still don't know what could have happened to the frame," Phoebe is saying into the phone, and after she hangs up, I notice something I hadn't before: Sam is already here, but he's skulking in the corner, looking even shadier than he normally does. (Which is very shady.)

"Phoebe, is Sam acting a little weird?" I think I'm starting to seem slightly paranoid asking.

"Weirder than usual, you mean?" says Phoebe. Normally, I wouldn't use the *W* word, and I don't think Phoebe would either. I've been called a weirdo before, so I'm a little sensitive to it—I know how much words like that can hurt. But in this case, I don't exactly think we're wrong. Sam is acting strange and he's gone out of his way to be nasty to us, so no, I don't trust him.

As Sam skulks off, I notice a piece of shiny paper sticking out of his pocket. It looks like the corner of the check that was in the display case along with the bike frame. The one that was supposed to fund a year's worth of training for the winner and entry into all the contests in this circuit. The check had a gold frame around the edges to match the bike.

Before I have time to think about what I'm doing, I'm riding after him. "Sam! Hang on a second!" I shout, and he looks over his shoulder, sees me riding toward him, and smirks.

I don't think about calling for Jen and Ali; I'm too busy starting to pedal really hard to catch up with him. It seems like he's looking toward the foam pit, but I don't know why he would be thinking about practicing in there right now. It's off-limits, like the rest of the jump lines, since the competition is starting soon.

So why would Sam be looking at it? My brain is speeding through scenarios, each one more comic-book-level dramatic than the last, none of them making sense. (Sam definitely didn't stash the bike in a pocket dimension, or time travel to after the competition to change the scores, for example.) But I know he was up to something, and I bet he took the bike.

Suddenly it hits me. The frame didn't leave Joyride, but it did get stolen. And then hidden. Sam buried it in the foam pit, probably hoping he could dig it out later and sneak it out of the park with no one noticing. And since he's not exactly a criminal mastermind, he's not even being subtle about it.

He must feel me staring at him, because he turns around and looks at me, staring at him and the foam pit. As we lock eyes, my superpowers finally seem to kick in, and I feel a surge of energy. He looks panicked, and I suddenly can see that he knows that I know what he did. And then he stops looking smug and starts racing toward the pit on his bike. I follow, my heart pounding so loud that I swear I can hear it.

As he gets closer, I'm not sure what he's planning to do—he can't leave with a frame without anyone seeing, but I don't think he's considered that. I have him running scared, and everyone knows that's when supervillains make mistakes. Sam's definitely made one: he didn't plan for the Shred Girls to be on the case this fast!

The jump that leads into the foam pit—the same one Phoebe made me do my first day in the park—is coming up. This time I'm going a lot faster, and I have way less control over the bike than I did that day. This may not have been a great idea.

But I'm already going faster than a speeding bullet, just like Superman but without the power of flight.

Sam is speeding toward it as well, and I'm closing in. We hit the ramp at almost the same moment, and I stop pedaling just early enough to let myself coast, up, up, up. . . .

At the last second, I remember to relax my body.

And suddenly, I'm airborne. Time feels like it's slowing down. I can hear some people shouting in the background. Maybe it's Phoebe; maybe it's Ali and Jen. I can see Sam, also in the air, looking completely out of control.

Instinctively, I lean toward him, pushing my bike out from under me and over to the other side, trying to make sure it doesn't land on him, or me. My legs kick out to the side, and I hang on to the handlebars tight, trying to keep a grip on the bike so I can land next to it, not on top of it, or have it hit Sam. Even if he is a jerk, I don't think hitting him with a steel bike frame is a good idea.

It's tempting, though. But what would Wonder Woman do?

(Answer: She probably would have just used her Lasso of Truth to get him to admit he took the frame. But since I don't have one, a chase scene seemed like the best option.)

We hit the foam at the same time, unscathed, and immediately start diving through the blocks, scrambling

to look for the frame. He shoves me out of the way, but I keep looking. My hand finally makes contact with something solid and decidedly not foam, and I grab on. Sam's hand locks around it a half second later, and we're in the middle of a vicious tug-of-war in the pit as he kicks and twists to try to grab the gold frame.

I hear shouting, and before I realize what's happening, someone has picked me up and is pulling me out of the pit, still hanging on to the bike. Matt has a grip on Sam, who's suddenly lost all his rabid energy and just looks angry and sullen.

The hand on my arm is Phoebe's, and she grabs me in a huge hug. "Holy moly, Linds! You just landed the coolest trick I've ever seen!" she shouts, seemingly oblivious to the bike frame. Her gaze catches on the shiny gold paint, and recognition dawns. "The frame!" she screams even louder.

Matt looks over, sees the frame, then looks back at Sam, who he's still holding by the arm. "You want to explain this?" he asks, and he sounds seriously mad.

"I just wanted to get the prize," Sam says, looking unapologetic, even angry that he got caught. He's still staring at the frame like he's about to develop telekinetic powers and move it with his mind.

But he doesn't get the chance. "Wait until I call your dad," Matt says, marching Sam off, and Sam glares as he walks past me. "You're in some serious trouble."

"Girls shouldn't be riding bikes anyway—they just get in the way," he snarls. "You're going to lose the contest, for sure."

"That's enough," Matt says through his teeth, pulling Sam along. "And, Lindsay, thanks."

"Sure," I say, but I'm furious, my hands are curled into fists, and I'm about to follow Matt in order to start screaming at Sam about just how wrong he is. Before I start stomping off, though, Phoebe turns to me.

"Umm, Lindsay?" She looks somewhat dumbfounded.

"Yeah?"

"Do you realize what you just did?"

I look over and see Jen and Ali sprinting toward me, shrieking. I can't really make out what they're saying (I think only dogs can hear pitches that high), but as they get closer and both hug me, I figure it's all good stuff. "That was an amazing jump!" Ali squeals.

"That's what I'm talking about," Phoebe practically shrieks. "You just managed to land a can-can and catch the bad guy all at once. It was amazing!"

"A what?" I ask, totally confused.

"It's a really advanced trick," Phoebe says.

"I still think you should have told us when you saw Sam," Jen grouses, but she doesn't look too upset. "Your hair is all messed up from the foam pit," she adds, grabbing a stray foam particle.

To make it a full party, Dave comes rushing over as

well, sweating, panting and—for once—looking as disheveled as I do.

"What happened? Are you okay?" he asks frantically, grabbing my shoulders and shaking me in a confused and worried panic. "What did Sam do?"

Phoebe winks at me over Dave's head.

"I'm fine," I start, but before I can tell him what happened, Ali, Jen, and even Phoebe are all talking over me, trying to explain.

"She chased down Sam and grabbed him in the foam pit—where he hid the frame," Phoebe says, talking the loudest.

"Yeah, but that's not the coolest part," Ali says over her. "She did an amazing air trick on the way down, just like a movie chase scene!"

"Actually, I was just trying to not hit Sam with my bike," I say, trying to downplay the trick. I mean, I'm sure I will never ever be able to replicate it.

⇛ Training Log ⇚

A couple of hours later, it's business as usual. The frame is back in the trophy case, Sam was escorted away by his parents, who we could all hear yelling at him from outside the office, Matt has calmed down, and Phoebe has been alternating between hugging and high-fiving me as she rushes around trying to keep everything organized.

I don't know what's going to happen to Sam, since the frame and check never technically left the park, so it's less of a theft and more of a prank, but Matt told his dad (and Phoebe told me) that he's banned for life from the park. Honestly? No one seems super disappointed by this news.

The competition itself feels a little anticlimactic at this point. I mean, I already caught a bad guy, so I'm floating on cloud nine. People keep congratulating me on nailing that trick—though I still don't really understand how I did it—and I'm having trouble focusing on the fact that my name will be called soon and I'll have to go roll through a jump line that I'm getting judged on. Ali and Jen are sitting on either side of me, but none of us are talking. Instead, they're watching the action, riveted, as they internally judge everyone else's tricks and think about how they'll stack up.

Superhero Tip: Even in a competition, while it's tempting to compare your abilities to everyone else's, you're only going to be able to do as good as you can do. Watching everyone else is fine, but it doesn't really matter for you. (Which is great advice Phoebe told me a few days ago, but really, really hard to do in real life.)

I just write to stay calm,

Lindsay

(Not very action-hero-y.)

CHAPTER 28

As names start to tick away, I realize that I'm on after two more riders. Suddenly, the nerves kick back in. What was I thinking?

Dave rolls by and stops behind me, his first run already completed and with plenty of time until the second. "You're going to be great," he says, patting my shoulder.

Agh. In all the excitement, I sort of forgot that he was going to be watching us.

Jen's name is called, and she turns white before stumbling up, tripping over her own feet. She clutches the handlebars like they're going to try to run away from her, and makes her way to the starting spot. I'm trying to pay attention and send positive vibes, but to be honest, I'm getting a little panicky myself now that I know that I'm up next.

Jen takes a deep breath and rolls down. She hits the first jump and actually gets some air, but comes down a little hard on the backside of the bump. She rallies and makes it over the second, and third, though her front wheel wobbles a bit at the top and she has to throw her weight forward to make it over. She takes one pedal stroke before the last bump but stops pedaling in time to make it over the jump cleanly. She loops around and rolls up to the top of platform again, high-fiving Phoebe and Ali as she rolls to a stop, looking slightly green and sick, but otherwise fine.

I spent so much time focusing on her that I almost missed the fact that I'm on deck—meaning I'm the next one to go after the guy who just rolled out. I jump up and grab my helmet, strapping it on in such a rush that there's a good chance I put it on backward. Phoebe walks over to me. "Ready?" she asks. My mouth is bone-dry and I don't think I can actually answer her, so I just nod.

She walks next to me as I walk my bike over to the start line, and the judges all smile and wave. I guess news of my stunt with Sam earlier has spread around the park, because they haven't smiled like that at any of the other competitors.

"Crush it," Phoebe whispers. She squeezes my shoulder and steps back.

I take a deep breath.

"Whenever you're ready," one judge says as the kid who just finished his set collapses on a bench, looking almost as drained as Jen.

I step onto my bike, put one foot on the pedal, and clutch my handlebars. I tell myself to breathe and relax. For a split second, I consider turning around and running away, but I can actually hear Ali, Jen, and Phoebe cheering for me. I have friends. They think I can handle this.

I think I can handle this.

I drop in. Thankfully, I manage to get my other foot onto my pedal and get three quick pedal strokes in before hitting the first of the four bumps. Up and over, nice and smooth, though no air. I push down to get more momentum on the backside of the bump, and when I crest over the second one, I have enough speed to lift my wheels just a bit above the surface. Two down. On the third, I get nervous and almost bobble at the top but push my front wheel forward to make it over without pedaling. I don't have enough time to start panicking before the fourth and last bump looms in front of me, so I push my weight into it and try to think light at the top. I manage to lift myself a couple of inches, but it feels like I'm getting a foot of air.

When my rear wheel touches down on the ground, I realize that I've made it. I survived! And I don't think I even did that badly!

The judges are at the top of the jumps when I get there, out of breath and my heart racing. They're smiling when I glance over, and I just know that I've advanced to the next round.

I can hear Dave cheering from the stands, but it's not just him—a few seats over from where he is, I see Phoebe's parents holding up a sign with my name on it. I can't believe they're here! (Tía Maria has a combination of terror and pride on her face, and I imagine this is hard for her to watch since she's so nervous about crashing.)

As I sit down, I glance over my shoulder and see Ali, looking grim and determined at the start line.

All of a sudden, a trio of voices boom out, "ALI!" and all of us jump—including poor Ali, who's already nervous enough. A herd of massive boys is making their way through the crowd, and even though a judge tries to protest their passage, they all swarm Ali and give her a huge group hug.

"I think those are her brothers," Jen whispers.

"Lucky her," I say, and I really do mean it—they form a wall around her and seem to just be projecting strength and excitement.

Unfortunately, Ali doesn't seem as psyched in the middle of the huddle. In fact, rather than seeming relieved to see familiar faces, she's turned a light shade of green. She looks more nervous than Jen and me combined—and we were pretty nervous.

The judge leans over and says, "It's your turn, Ali," and she swallows hard.

Her brothers shift from the group hug and gather right at the finishing platform, loudly calling her name and hooting. I'm both jealous that she has brothers who seem to be excited for her, and glad that I didn't have a cheering section–slash–peanut gallery when I had my turn.

She almost stutters as she starts—I can see her foot twitch before it lands safely on the pedal—but she's off. That nervous energy must have helped, because she's going just a bit faster than we've done in practice, and when she hits the first bump, she pops up in the air, just hovering slightly over the jump before precisely landing on the backside.

"Textbook perfect," I hear one brother say to another, surprised.

The next jump is even higher, and the third is equally well done. She pumps her arms heading down the back of that one and pulls her body up for the last jump, going higher than any of the guys did on the three-foot bump. The crowd—her brothers especially—goes wild.

She seems stunned when she gets back on the platform and steps off her bike, especially since her trio of burly brothers bum-rush her for more bear hugs. Ten minutes later, when the judges tack up the score sheet from round one, I'm too scared to look, so Jen and Ali go over together. They return, grinning from ear to ear.

"We made it!" Jen declares, and we start jumping up and down. Again, this is new for me. I've never squealed or jumped up and down with a group of girlfriends in my entire life, but you know what? It feels right. Phoebe bounces over and joins in the jumping, telling us that she's super proud of how far we've come.

Suddenly, it hits me. We're going to have to do this all again, on bigger jumps, in an hour. Instead of being nervous, I'm just thrilled.

A few minutes later, when the excitement has finally

started to wear off, I'm sitting on a bench hidden away from everyone, shaking a little and trying to keep my cool. Speaking of cool, Phoebe pops up behind me and leans over the bench.

"How are you doing?" she asks sympathetically. "You've had a pretty crazy day!"

"Well, I was good before, but now I'm getting a little nervous," I admit, trying to look casual even as I feel like I could vomit everywhere.

"It's scary, isn't it?" she says, and I nod. "You know, I feel the same way when I do these competitions too. But didn't it feel awesome finishing that last round?"

I nod again.

"The thing is, if you don't do the scary stuff, it's way harder to get that feeling," she says. "Besides, chasing down Sam and doing that crazy trick was way harder than these bigger jumps, trust me."

Ali and Jen roll up on their bikes, cutting off our heart-to-heart. Ali slumps down beside me, looking exhausted. "Tough day?" Phoebe asks.

"My brothers are here," Ali replies weakly, as though that explains everything.

"And they were cheering like crazy!" Jen says. "I don't get why you're so bummed about it. I love it when I have a cheering section. . . . I kind of miss it, actually. You're lucky!"

"It's just that they've always been really hard to impress, and I've never been able to get as good as they are," Ali says.

"Wait a second," Phoebe interjects. "Your brother is Joe Deign, right?"

Ali nods.

"Ha!" Phoebe barks out a laugh. "You think he's always been that good? I was in a competition with him a few years ago, and he bobbled so hard on the first round that he fell off the jump!"

Ali looks stunned. "Seriously?" she asks.

"Seriously. You don't get as good as your brothers without taking a few spills," Phoebe explains. "That's all part of it. So even if they're being tough on you, they're just trying to help, in their own really, truly, incredibly dumb way."

Jen jumps in: "Also, they probably smell awful."

"That too," Phoebe says thoughtfully. And just as we all seem like we're calmed down, we hear our names being called over the loudspeaker. Everyone in round two is to line up at the platform for the next set. We all look at each other, panicked.

"Girls," Phoebe says, a teensy bit impatiently. "You got this."

We all clasp hands again, before hopping onto our bikes and pedaling toward the platform. As we roll up,

Ali's brothers pat her on the back excitedly. Dave, standing across the platform, gives me a crooked grin. And an older couple wearing matching Joyride T-shirts, looking almost as tiny as some of the really young riders, are holding up a sign that says, "Go, Jen!"

"My grandparents," she explains. "I tried to tell them they wouldn't fit in with the crowd here, but they insisted on coming anyway."

"They're awesome," says Phoebe enthusiastically. "I think it's great that they're here."

And it really is. Except maybe in the next thirty seconds, when her grandmother reaches over and yanks up one boy's dropping jeans. "I can see your underpants," she squawks.

"Grandma!" Jen hisses furiously.

"What?" she asks, all innocent. Behind her, Jen's grandfather looks like he's trying not to laugh.

The judges call up the first rider, who—thankfully—isn't any of us. I watch him take off and, after a slight bobble on the first bump, make a strong recovery as he hits the next three jumps with finesse. That makes me feel better about my chances. I don't have to do anything earth-shattering, just reasonably controlled. I can handle that. Controlled. Collected. Like how Catwoman would be facing down Batman. I've totally got this.

Jen is called next, and her grandparents get even louder,

despite her frantic hushing noises as she heads to the line. She stares down the steep drop-off that starts the set. Jen looks a little paralyzed while also managing to look like she's about to throw up. It isn't a pretty picture, and just seeing her face makes me clench in sympathy, and nerves.

"You can do it, snookums!" cheers her grandfather. Ali stifles a giggle—I can tell she's relieved not to be the only one with embarrassing family present. But before we can start giggling too much, Jen has dropped in and she's heading up the first jump, and we're holding our collective breath.

She makes a slight bobble at the top and only lifts her front wheel off the ground, but she comes down the backside of the bump smoothly. She hits the next one a lot better, getting a few inches off the ground and looking a little less rigid.

By the third one, she tries to show off, and that's when she botches the lift, slamming her wheel down a bit hard on the backside. Her last jump is pretty tiny and she just barely gets air, but it's clean otherwise.

She rolls back up on the platform, drops her bike, and hurls herself into her grandfather's arms, who hugs her tightly. I've never seen her get emotional, but it's obvious how much she loves her grandparents and how much they love her. Her grandma has enveloped both of them in her arms. I can see tears in her eyes. I don't think Jen will win, but it looks like her grandparents are about as proud of her now as they would be if she took home a gold medal.

Ali is starting to look green again, since she's up in a couple of minutes, and Phoebe comes over to pat her back and whisper a few words of encouragement.

She's sweating even before she starts, lining up and wiping her forehead on her sleeve. And then the judge blows the whistle. Ali doesn't hesitate for a second, just dives in.

And she absolutely nails it.

It's the best run of the day. Phoebe is shrieking, and so are Jen and I. Ali hits all four jumps, using her momentum to pop up both wheels into the air, and doesn't even need to push the pedals slightly to keep her momentum going. She's got a natural flow, and it looks beautiful. She doesn't look like the nervous girl who started the run anymore—she looks calm and confident.

When she pops back onto the platform, she smiles so wide that I think her face is going to crack, and this time when her brothers rush her and start hugging her and shouting, she doesn't look terrified. She looks stoked.

The kid who drops in as Ali is still getting hugged looks ultra-confident, and for good reason. He might technically be a beginner, but he clearly has some serious skills. He looks effortless as he glides up and over, with casual jumps at the top of each bump. It's pretty clear that he's going to be a top contender by the way the judges are murmuring and smiling, and I'm prepared to hate him for stealing Ali's thunder. But when he finishes and looks relieved and also nervous enough to throw up, I realize that he's just as scared as I am. . . . Maybe even more, since clearly he has a ton of natural talent, and a lot more to prove. I'll feel good if I finish this without falling over, but it's obvious that he knows he's good and wants to do well. He kind of reminds me of Jen—come to think of it, maybe they should hang out.

Jen does seem to be staring pretty hard at him, and I can't tell if she's jealous, if she wants him to give her some pointers, or if she's developed a crush. Possibly it's all three.

And then it occurs to me that, in about ninety seconds, I'm going to have to drop in, and the fear strikes again. Is this going to happen every single time I compete? I'm not sure whether this makes things better or worse, but once again, my knees feel like jelly, like when I'm going over a particularly bumpy section of pavement on the bike. I can actually feel my stomach turning. It's not a great sensation—I wish they provided barf bags on the platform like they do on planes.

I walk my way to the starting grid like someone who's about to walk the plank. I mean, really, other than the bike involved, it's kind of a similar thing. This is starting to seem a little cruel and inhuman. Phoebe waggles her eyebrows, and if you ask me, she does it kind of villain-ously.

I can tell that the judges are about to signal my start. When I hear the high-pitched shriek, I drop in.

It's not my smoothest tiny hop at the top of the first whoop, but it's certainly not my worst. Honestly, I'd say it's in the top ten. I don't get a lot of air, but my wheels come off the ground and I land at a perfectly straight angle, so I smoothly roll into the second without any problems. In fact, my second one is even better, even though I can hear the blood rushing in my head.

I actually get both wheels off the ground slightly higher and land it neatly again, going fast enough that the third bump feels like I'm flying. I almost bobble as I touch down, and I'm sure the judges noticed me tense up, but I think I recovered smoothly enough, since I clear the fourth and final bump with no problems. Dimly, I realize that Phoebe is shouting my name, and she's gotten the crowd to join in.

When I roll onto the deck, sweaty, shaking, and com-pletely wiped out, I realize two things: (1) that people I don't know are still chanting my name, and this has never ever happened to me before, and (2) I'm done. Finally. And while I thought I was going to throw up this morn-ing, and I still very well might, I actually had what could be considered fun. In a weird, weird way.

Ali and Jen rush me and I'm enveloped in yet another

big group hug (I could get used to this). When Phoebe joins in, I let my bike topple over behind me, dropping it exactly like she told me not to. We're all jumping up and down and squealing.

"You were amazing!" Jen yells.

"You were fantastic!" I yell back at her.

"We're all pretty awesome!" Ali shouts, and then it sinks in.

I'm finally part of a team.

Training Log

We're waiting together as the judges confer on their scores. In the other room, we can see the pizza party being set up, and I'm finally feeling hungry again. But food is a long way off—they still have to do the advanced competition, and, of course, the prizes get handed out. Sure, I'm getting a little ahead of myself, but still, I can't wait for it to be over. . . . I'm starving, and I'm definitely ready to party! And I'm also not very patient, as it turns out. Waiting for results is harder than competing!

> **Superhero Tip:** I feel like I write about food a lot in this journal—superheroes and cyclists need to eat a lot to fuel their training. A hungry superhero isn't a happy superhero.

I'd rather be snacking,
Lindsay
(A little too Shaggy from *Scooby-Doo*.)

CHAPTER 29

Jen, Ali, and I huddle on the bench. We're just waiting for the judges to put the final list on the wall. We're pretty sure Ali's got it in the bag. She's at least got to be on the podium in the top three.

Dave did swing by to high-five us all and winked at me when it was my turn—which Phoebe definitely noticed, judging by the smirk she gave me after. But now he's over with some friends, probably glad that Sam isn't there and that his race went well. He finished fifth in a really big field—fifty guys competing—so I can tell he's pretty happy. Which is good, because I'm hoping to be calm and collected enough to have a real conversation with him later, one where I'm not just stammering along.

While I'm daydreaming, I miss the fact that the judges have stopped consulting one another and are moving to post a piece of paper on the bulletin board. I'm clammy with sweat.

We all rush over to look, and the first thing that hits me is a huge wave of disappointment when I see that none of us won. It's some kid named Jeremy, who I guess was the guy who went right before me who rode so smoothly on everything.

But as my eyes go slightly farther down, they almost

pop out of my head. There's Ali in second place, Jen in fifth. . . . My eyes start to blur before I can find my name. Phoebe rushes behind me, practically shoving me into the board in her hurry to look.

And then I see it. My name, in third place. I got third. I got third!

I feel a punch on my shoulder—it's Phoebe, and she spins me around and grabs me in a huge hug. "You killed it!" she shouts, and Ali and Jen are right behind her. Jen's looking a little less excited, but she's still smiling, so I guess we're okay.

"Can't win 'em all," she says, but adds, "I'll get you both next time, though."

It's a great feeling—but before we get a minute to really process it, the advanced competitors are being called up to get in line, and next to me, Phoebe does something surprising.

She pulls a total Clark Kent move, peeling off her sweatshirt to reveal a Phoebe and the Chainbreakers T-shirt with a competition number pinned to it, and elbow pads already in place. She hands me her sweatshirt and just says, "Hold this for a second, okay?"

We all just stare as she walks over and grabs her bike from the bike rack, tugs on her helmet, and pedals over to the start platform at the top of the biggest jump line in the park. The guy holding the microphone reading competitors' names starts talking again. "First up, we have . . ."

He pauses. "Umm . . . Phoebe Gomez?" He seems confused, probably because there aren't any other women up on the platform and Phoebe is surrounded by big guys.

Phoebe rolls up and gives him a fierce grin. She looks directly at me and winks, and then takes two pedal strokes before dropping in, down a nearly vertical fifteen-foot wooden cliff. She pumps her arms as she hits the top of the first massive jump, pushes the bike high into the air, and whips the back end out from under her for a split second, before coming onto it just as she touches down on the other side of the jump. On the second roller, as she goes airborne she keeps her feet on the pedals, but shoots her arms out like she's Superman midflight. And when she hits the last one and jumps, she kicks out her legs straight behind her, then brings them back down, smoothly hits the bottom of the jump, and pops onto the deck. She smiles and casually sits down as the guy whose

name just got called stares at her with his mouth hanging open.

The crowd goes completely and totally wild. I glance over to the stands. Tía Maria is covering her eyes, Tío Carlos is standing and screaming, and their sign that had my name has been flipped and Phoebe's name is in huge letters.

I wonder if I'll ever be able to do jumps like that.

Jen nudges me.

"I know you decided it was all in your head, but are you positive your cousin doesn't have superpowers?" she asks, looking completely, deadly serious.

≋ Training Log ≋

I can't believe how good Phoebe was—I had no idea she could ride like that. I also can't believe that I'm waiting to be called up to the podium.

> **Superhero Tip:** It's good to have a mentor like Phoebe, who can teach you how to do cool stuff . . . and is still doing cool stuff on her own. Basically, find someone you want to be when you grow up, and try to make them teach you whatever they can.

Now the top five finishers are all standing on the stage, so I'm huddled with Jen (who has since fixed her hair and added lip gloss, and looks ridiculously cool, as usual), and Ali, who is flanked by her brothers and grinning from ear to ear as they keep telling her how great she did. I'm just kicking the ground, writing this, and waiting for it to be over while Phoebe is huddled talking to the promoters, judges, and Matt. I know how strange it looks that I'm sitting here writing while the other kids who did well are playing on their phones or posing for pictures with their friends, but, hey, this is how I stay calm. Even superheroes need a security blanket, and this journal is mine. Right now the idea of standing in front of people seems terrifying. What if I fall over? It could happen.

Klutzy forever,
Lindsay
(I guess not entirely true after today!)

CHAPTER 30

Phoebe hops up onto the stage gracefully, microphone in hand, smiling at me as if urging me to calm down a little. After the applause for her finally dies down, she introduces the event, adding that next year, she's going to make sure that the girls have their own race—and the judges all are standing to the side, smiling and nodding in agreement.

"People sometimes ask why girls need their own race— why not just make them compete with the boys?" she says. "But that's not fair to the girls and women who ride. We're built different; we have different strengths and different limitations. While racing all as one group might seem equal, it's not equitable. We want three women on a podium, three men on a separate one. We want girls to see someone who looks like them standing on the top step."

Judging by the applause and cheers she's getting as she talks, I don't think she's going to have much of a fight on her hands.

"I admit, we didn't seem to need it today, but it seems like it's only fair that the boys have a chance to get on the podium too!" she adds. The crowd laughs, and I can tell Phoebe is psyched that she didn't get booed for the sentiment. All the boys and parents seem to be pretty in favor of a girls' race—and I don't think it's just because the boys are bummed to get beaten by girls. We pretty clearly showed them that girls are at the park, ready to race—at any level. Hopefully, next competition, we'll have even more beginner girls, in our own category that we deserve because we're showing up.

Phoebe starts calling the top five riders in the beginner category, starting with Jen in fifth place. She walks up a little sheepishly but breaks into a huge smile once Phoebe puts a medal around her neck. Steve, one of the quiet guys who's always there practicing—and whom I've seen chatting with Phoebe a few times—gets called up next in fourth. Then it's my turn.

"Lindsay isn't just a great rider—she and her friends were real-life superheroes today," Phoebe says, instead of just calling my name. "And I couldn't be more proud of my cousin."

When I walk to the podium, she grabs me in a big hug, the crowd is cheering, and I'm blinking back tears. She puts the medal around my neck, and I hop onto the third-place spot.

As Phoebe hands second—Ali!—and first place their medals, Penguin pops his head out of the backpack at Phoebe's feet and puts his paws in the air, begging for snacks. "You should probably follow his lead," Phoebe laughs, and all of us on the stage raise our arms up.

I've never won anything before, and my arms are definitely not used to this position, but I think I could get comfortable here. I look over, and Ali still looks slightly stunned to be in second place, while Jen happily and graciously waves at the crowd like she's done this a hundred times before (which she probably has).

"Can we get a photo of just the girls?" one photographer in the crowd shouts, and the guys leave the podium as the three of us crowd onto one step. Jen and I flank Ali, and we all join hands. I'm not surprised that Ali is as sweaty as I am; she seems just as nervous. Our arms go up, and we're all smiling like we'll never stop.

"This group of girls is going to go far," Matt says into the microphone. "And I'm so glad I can say that they got their start here at Joyride."

After we've walked down and joined the crowd, I get another surprise for the day. As I'm standing next to my bike and admiring my medal, someone taps me on the shoulder. I turn around and register blond hair, jean shorts, and a purple tank top, but it takes me a second before I realize that it's Dana, the coolest girl in my school, standing there.

"Hey, Lindsay," she says, smiling.

"Umm, hi—what are you doing at a bike park?" I ask, completely confused and a little more abrupt than was probably polite. But then again, she's never spoken to me before, and we've been in school together since first grade.

"My brother competed," she says, pointing at a guy who's deep in conversation with a few other riders. "I saw your jumps too—you were so cool!"

Hold on a second. Did the coolest girl in school just say I was cool? Did I jump into an alternate reality when I took that last run?

"Thanks," I manage to say back. (So smooth!)

"Maybe you could teach me how to ride in here some-time?" she asks, seeming completely sincere. "I didn't know other girls rode here. I just figured it was all guys."

While part of me wants to tell her absolutely not, and the Shred Girls are an exclusive club, and we don't need any other girls to join, I know that's not the right answer. That's a supervillain-level answer. I look over at Phoebe, talking with Ali and Jen, and I realize that Shred Girls shouldn't just be the three of us.

"Sure," I find myself saying. "Give me your number and I'll text you when we're going to be here next. We'll get you riding better than your brother."

She laughs. "I would love that," she says, and grabs my phone and programs her number in. Her brother is wav-ing at her, so she says goodbye and heads out, but only after she makes me promise that I will text.

Maybe this whole making-friends thing isn't so tough after all.

Training Log

After all the drama, it feels like we're having an epilogue to a really intense action-adventure movie. Which, come to think of it, was sort of what I've been waiting for this whole time. It's been a big day—and it's pretty sweet that all of us have medals to show for it. Phoebe won her category by a huge margin, so there will be a gold frame in her apartment, and maybe I can even borrow it sometime. You know, for motivational purposes.

Superhero Tip: Batman will probably never loan out the Batmobile, but a girl can dream.

Tío Carlos and Tía Maria both couldn't stop talking about how proud they were, and Tía Maria called my parents, who were shrieking so loud with excitement that I had to hold the phone at arm's length for a full thirty seconds. Phoebe was even more thrilled, since Tío Carlos told her he supposed her little BMX bike was just as good as a road bike . . . and admitted that he never won a trophy quite as cool as this frame. But now they're gone and the party room is rocking, with Phoebe's band playing a set at the front of the room, pizza still being served (thankfully!), and everyone laughing and talking, showing off tricks on their bikes, wheelie-ing around, and, off their bikes, dancing. I'm sitting in a corner, taking it all in, and breathing for a second.

Epically yours,
Lindsay
(I like it!)

CHAPTER 31

Dave walks toward me, a slice of pizza in each hand. He grins and moves to give me a high five, but catches himself when the pizza threatens to fall off the plate. He offers me the plate ruefully instead.

He brought me pizza?

"Do you want to dance?" he asks abruptly, and tosses his half-eaten pizza into the trash, just barely making it in. He's a BMXer and not a basketball player for a reason, I guess.

I'm standing there, not sure what to do, since he just handed me a slice of pizza. I'm not really sure how to dance while I hold it at the same time. Is this really how the movie ends? Suddenly, it's gone from action-adventure to comedy, and I'm feeling really silly. Dave seems to notice, so he takes the pizza back from me, which is an infinitely weirder move.

He sets it down on the table. "Now do you want to dance?" he asks, and I nod. Normally, I would be terrified (boys! dancing!), but after today's adventure with the stolen bike and then in the competition, this seems tame by comparison. I can see Jen and Ali in the corner of my eye, dancing away on the floor and going a little crazy. He grabs my hand and pulls me over toward the band, and I catch Phoebe's eye. Her face breaks out in a huge grin, and she gives me a quick thumbs-up between guitar plucks.

As we get on the floor, the song they're playing ends, but Phoebe keeps smiling as she mouths something to the singer. "We're going to slow it down a little for this next song," she says before they burst into a funky, faster version of a cheesy Frank Sinatra song that I know my parents love dancing to, and Dave grabs my hand and pulls me to the middle of the floor. Next to me, Ali and Jen are dancing together and checking out a few of Dave's friends, who seem to be having an eating contest in the corner. A lot of the other kids from the race today are bopping around, pretending they know how to waltz. Dave pulls me into a clumsy dance move and steps on my foot, but manages to get his one hand on my waist.

"I don't know how to waltz," he yells over the music.

"I can see that," I yell back, but I can't stop smiling. "Want to try salsa?" Finally, those moves my mom made me practice as a kid are paying off, and we rock somewhat in time with the beat. We're not great, but at least Dave can shuffle along with my moves. (Phoebe nods approvingly from the stage—her mom made her take the same lessons, so she knows what I'm up to.)

Now it's a proper movie ending. Even when the song is over, he keeps holding my hand, and I see Jen and Ali looking over and whispering to each other. But I'm paying way more attention to Dave.

"Did I mention that you did awesome today?" he asks.

"You did, a few times," I reply. "But you can say it again if you want."

Look at that, I made it through a full sentence—and it was actually almost witty!

"Well, you did awesome," he says. "Want to eat that pizza?"

"Absolutely." I smile wide, and he keeps my hand in his as we walk back toward the tables.

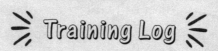

Training Log

Transmission from the girls' locker room: success! I didn't break Dave's feet, ankles, or other appendages. And I think he actually liked dancing with me! Fantastic!

> **Superhero Tip:** Thank your parents for dance lessons you hated as a kid. As a superhero, you may be called on to be agile or blend in at a salsa club at a moment's notice.

Yayyyyyyyy.
Lindsay
(Definitely, positively no.)

CHAPTER 32

Thankfully, it's a little quieter now that the band has decided to take a break. Dave and I sit down at one of the tables so I can eat my now stone-cold slice of pepperoni pizza. Luckily, I prefer it cooled off, so, really, that dance party worked in more ways than one.

As we're sitting, I realize we've been talking for twenty minutes and I haven't once run out of things to say, gotten shy, or forgotten my own name. We're just . . . talking.

Phoebe walks up with a guy in tow.

"Dave, I see you've met Phoebe's cousin," the mystery man says.

Phoebe's cheeks are bright red, and she's wearing a sweet smile that I've never seen before. "Lindsay, this is Ben—my boyfriend."

"And you already know my brother, Dave," Ben says, sticking out a hand for me to shake. Wait—Phoebe is dating Dave's brother? And he's cute too. He looks like an older version of Dave, with shorter dark brown hair and big brown eyes, and he's wearing a button-down flannel in black and gray with streaks of teal, with black jeans. He puts his arm around Phoebe's waist, and the two of them just look at us, grinning like my parents did when I left for school for the first time. No wonder she knew so much about Dave!

But I guess it's okay, since I realize I'm looking at Phoebe the same way, even though Dave's arm isn't around me (sigh). I had no idea she had a boyfriend, and that he'd be so, well, regular. I was expecting someone . . . more pierced. He does have a lot of scars on his hands, but I'm guessing that's from crashing his bike, not from terrorizing puppies or whatever it is supervillains do.

"You did great today," he says, looking right at me. I feel a little like a deer in headlights, but I recover enough to mumble a quick thanks. Then he turns to Phoebe and shocks me even more. "Do you think Lindsay, Ali, and Jen could come train at my gym sometime? I'd love to test them."

Test us for what? Superpowers?

But I realize that he must mean our riding. And while that would have bummed me out a few weeks ago, today I'm excited by the idea of him testing our riding skills. "It won't be as much fun as riding around here," he adds. "You'd be on stationary bikes and we'd do some work with weights, but it'll get you even better at riding when you are here. You're good enough that you should be adding in stuff other than practicing the exact same jumps all the time."

"That would be cool," I say, trying to act casual. Jen and Ali pop up behind my shoulder too, having walked over at the sound of their names.

"You want to coach us?" Ali asks eagerly, looking like she wants to record him saying it, probably to play back to her brothers. One is over in the corner talking to another girl who was in the contest. I assume he's giving her some pointers, but I somehow doubt he's being very helpful. The others seem to be going through as much pizza as they can.

"Well, Phoebe will still be coaching your technical skills here—no one is better than her," Ben says, smiling a little sappily at my cousin. "But yeah, I'd handle the more fitness-based side of things."

"I'll have to talk to my other coach, but that sounds kind of cool," Jen says. I know she just wants to brag that she has another coach, and I don't blame her.

The more I spend time with her, the more I realize that she's insecure and maybe even a little scared. Well, maybe she's not that scared of me. But she's definitely scared of something.

"We'll talk about it more later," Ben says.

"Then we're going to go dance!" Jen says, and grabs me with one hand and Ali with the other, dragging us back to the kids still dancing in the corner. I jump around with Ali while Jen tries to show off some dance moves,

but she eventually gives up once she sees that her sway-
ing arms and intricate moves are scaring off the boys.
She joins in with us instead, bouncing around, smiling
and laughing.

Dave and I dance a few more times, and I'm still mar-
veling at the fact that his brother is going to be my coach
and is dating my cousin. Talk about weird coincidences!

By the end of the party, I'm practically falling asleep
on my backpack, but Ali, Jen, Dave, and a couple of his
friends are sitting in the corner with me, making big plans
and talking about competitions that they'd love to do.
There's one out on the West Coast that sounds epic, and
I can't wait to get home and start researching what we
should do next.

Ali's brothers haven't left the party either, and every
time it quiets down, they interrupt each other to tell stories about crazy jump lines they've ridden. They seem
a little full of themselves, but they do sound like fun.
I can see why Ali gets so nervous about living up to
what they've done—from what they say, they've raced
all around the world, been on TV and in magazines, and
toured with a big team. If I were Ali, I'd be intimidated
by them too.

But it gets late fast—it's been a long day, and soon
we're the only ones left other than Matt, who's been trying to clean up pizza boxes and soda cans for the last
hour. Before we head out, we help him drag the recycling

bins outside, and he hugs Phoebe and thanks all of us before stumbling back into the building. I bet he sleeps on his desk tonight.

When we all say good night, it doesn't feel like goodbye, even though the competition is over. We've got way too much planned to quit now.

Training Log

Since the competition last week, it feels like everything has changed. Today, for example, I'm sitting outside in Phoebe's front yard, watching Dave mess around on his bike in the driveway. Jen and Ali are flanking me as we lounge in the shade under a tree, sipping the kombucha that Phoebe made and Ben mixed with ice and lemonade. Even Jen likes it! I'm not finding as much time to write now that I actually have friends. (I have friends!) Mom will be happy about that anyway. Still, don't think I've forgotten about this training journal. I actually saw Ali looking at it the other day when it was sticking out of my backpack, and I think she was kind of interested. Not that I would let her read it, of course. Maybe someday.

I promised the girls I was just writing down a quick entry, so I'll make this brief. I can't quite believe that this is my real life. It's pretty exciting—but even with the competition, the movie-worthy dance scene, and all that stuff, the normal daily living with Phoebe isn't hectic. We train, we eat, we talk and hang out. And that's sort of the best part.

Superhero Tip: Enjoy the ride—sometimes literally! Day-to-day practice isn't automatically condensed into a training montage, but I'm starting to realize that you have to appreciate the stuff that happens between the panels of the comic book. That white space is where the relaxing and the real fun happens.

Chilling out,
Lindsay
(Factual, but not a great sign-off.)

CHAPTER 33

Ali and I are flipping through my comic book collection, and Jen is casually flipping through one of Phoebe's fashion magazines, trying to keep it under wraps so Phoebe won't snatch it back. But Phoebe's not paying attention to us at all—she's too preoccupied laughing at something Ben said while she tosses the Frisbee to Penguin. Penguin, for the record, is not great at Frisbee, but then again, his legs are only about four inches long. It's hard for him to get a lot of speed. Every so often Ali asks me a question about one of my comic books, or Jen stops to point at a cool outfit in the magazine (most of them look like superhero costumes anyway, all tights and spandex). I'm laughing and joking along with them.

It's been a good summer.

The only problem is, I don't want it to end. I think Phoebe and Ben have been scheming. Real-life scheming, not supervillain stuff. He's been over a lot more often, and I've seen them in the park's office and on the phone tons lately. I know Jen and Ali want to stay for the rest of the summer, maybe longer, but I don't know when they both have to go home. We're just hoping Ben can start working with us and Phoebe before then. We have a lot of work to do if we're going to win the intermediate competition next year. The official team name: Shred Girls, of course!

"How many days left?" Ali asks. I know what she means: we're getting closer and closer to when we'll all be going home, and I'm sad even thinking about my new friends leaving.

"Unless I change my parents' minds, I only have eleven days left," sighs Jen. "I never thought I'd say this, but I don't want to leave you weirdos."

Huh. Maybe being a weirdo isn't so bad, because it sounds nice the way she's saying it!

Mom and Dad are coming home soon, and while I'll be happy to see them again, I'm really going to miss staying with Phoebe. But now that we're friends and she's coaching me, I should see her more. I've already talked to my parents about it, although they kept repeating, "Wait, what?" when I tried to tell them about the competition. I think they couldn't wrap their heads around me doing a sport—let alone doing well in it. Or maybe they thought I had gone crazy this summer and imagined the whole thing.

Either way, they eventually understood. I think they're even going to let me stay with Phoebe a couple of days a week for the rest of the summer so that I can keep training with her, and luckily, she seems to actually want me here.

"Linds, I can see you thinking from here. Calm it

down," she says from where she and Ben are sitting, having exhausted poor Penguin with Frisbee overload. I jerk out of my thinking position, while Penguin remains lying on his side, panting heavily.

"I was just wondering . . . why did you decide to hang out with me this summer? You didn't have to," I say.

"Lindsay . . ." Phoebe shakes her head. "I know it's a little weird, especially since you thought I was a super-villain for the first week," she says. "And, hey, I wasn't really sure how this summer would go either. I didn't know if we'd get along, or if I'd be shipping you off to Estonia on an express flight."

"Really?" I ask, curious. She was as nervous as I was?

"Really," she says. "But clearly, I didn't have much to worry about—I think we worked together just fine."

She gestures to herself and then me, and I realize that we're wearing pretty much the same thing: leggings and a T-shirt from Joyride. Our hair is even pulled back in braids. Since the start of the summer, her hair has gotten lighter, almost the same shade of brown as mine, and since I've grown a bit more in the last couple of months, now we're not even that different in height. We really do look more like sisters than cousins. Or a superhero and supervillain. Maybe I needed to grow into it. And maybe she did too.

Either way, it's pretty great. "Well, thanks," I say. "Really. I've had the best summer."

"Me too," says Phoebe. "So . . ." She trails off.

I know what's coming. I'm freaked out about going back home, even though I miss my parents. Ali and Jen and I have been trying to figure out how we're going to stay together as a team—Phoebe made some vague noise about starting a program for us at Joyride, but so far, nothing official has come of it.

"What?" I ask, suspicious. "Are you kicking me out?"

She laughs. "Actually, it's the opposite. I talked to your parents, Jen's parents, and Ali's parents about a plan Ben and I came up with. But before I say anything else, tell me something: How serious are you about riding? Do you love it?"

I'm stumped for a second. Earlier this summer, I would have said absolutely not, and why the heck would I want to ride a bike at all, let alone over a bunch of weird jumps. But that was before I met the girls, before I managed to jump . . . before I realized that I didn't need to be anything but myself to have fun in the bike park with my friends. And it was before I could bunny hop, or hold a plank for a minute straight. And way before another girl my age stopped me at the park to ask where I got my cool shirt and helmet.

"I really, really love it," I say honestly.

"Great. Because Ben and I worked out a plan, and we're hoping you guys will be excited about it. There's a big bike park on the West Coast that I think you guys would love, with a huge training center. You three are a little young for the programs that the actual cycling association puts on, but Ben and I convinced them that the two of us could host a mini camp for you girls and a few others this August that will finish with another competition." She pauses to catch her breath. "What do you think?"

I can't believe it. The three of us—four, if you count Phoebe—spending the rest of the summer riding bikes and hanging out on the West Coast? "That sounds amazing," I say. "Do you really think we're good enough?"

"We've been showing people that security-camera video of you catching Sam, plus the footage of all of you at the competition, and a lot of them think the three of you could be really good with a little more work," she replies. "Your parents think it would be great for you. Between us, they seem a little too excited. I think they think you're shy or something. No idea why," she adds playfully.

"Beats me," I say, and duck behind my comic book as Phoebe tosses a piece of ice from her glass at me.

"So you're in?" she asks.

"Definitely!" I say, practically squealing it.

"Great. Ali and Jen?" The two of them were clearly eavesdropping, and they basically fall over themselves to rush toward us and shout yes.

"Oh, and we'll be staying in Ali's dad's house for the

month, since it's right near the bike park," Phoebe adds casually. "So get used to having brothers."

Oh boy.

By the time we drive over to the park for an afternoon practice session, my head is spinning with all the ideas Phoebe has for training. She has a whole plan already worked out with Ben, and I can't believe that they're going to spend all this time making us better.

The three of us hit the pump track first to warm up, like we always do, but it's even more exciting now. We're a team! (Or a league, in superhero lingo.)

"Shred Girls forever," says Ali as we pause at the top of the track, and she puts her hands out for high fives.

"Shred Girls!" we all yell, and it bounces off the walls in an echo. People turn and stare a bit, but I don't care. Let them watch!

"Let's ride," I say, grabbing my bike, and the three of us spin off toward the jump lines. We have a lot of practicing to do.

〰 Training Log 〰

So. This summer I learned how to ride a bike, solve a crime, make new friends, talk to a boy, and dress in a style that's all me. Riding the bike was definitely the best part. Or maybe the friends. Heck, the pizza was pretty great too. It's been a crazy summer, and I can't wait to start my next journal out on the West Coast. This is the last page I have in this diary, so it's time to wrap it up and say goodbye for now. I'll write again soon!

Shred Girls forever,
Lindsay
(Now, *that* feels right.)

Shred Girls

How Cyclists Are
Basically Superheroes

1. They wear funny clothes in bright colors, with kind of ridiculous logos—and sometimes, like Superman's alter ego, Clark Kent, they even hide the spandex parts under baggy clothes.
2. They fly (though for cyclists, I don't think that's always a good thing—like right before they crash).
3. They have kind of silly (but important) headgear.
4. They're all helping to save the world—but cyclists do it by cutting down on pollution caused by driving!
5. They have super-muscular legs.
6. Sometimes they really can save the day.

Glossary

Bike riding is super fun, but it can be intimidating at first . . . not just because of the riding, but because of all the crazy new words you're going to hear tossed around! Don't worry—you'll pick up on the lingo really quick once you get riding. But why wait? If you had a great time reading about Lindsay, Ali, and Jen, here's a guide to all the cool things they do and see at Joyride:

Berm: A banked curve on a track, used for maintaining speed and smooth cornering.

BMX: An abbreviation for "bicycle motocross," a style of bike riding and racing.

Bunny hop: A trick in which the rider lifts both wheels off the ground at once.

Case: Hitting the back wheel of the bike on an obstacle that one is trying to clear.

Drop-in: The act of approaching a feature. One would "drop in" on a jump line.

Feature: Any human-made obstacle in a park.

Foam pit: A pit that riders go off and land in. Similar to a ball pit in a kids' play place, it's used for practicing tricks and jumps.

Freeride: A style of BMX focusing more on tricks and style than speed.

J-Hop: A trick in which the rider lifts first the front wheel and then the rear wheel.

Jump line: A straight line of rollers similar to the ones on the pump track, but higher, intended to get the rider some air while going over them.

Manual: Riding a wheelie without pedaling.

Pump track: An oval-shaped track with bermed corners and rollers spaced throughout, which can be ridden by "pumping" instead of pedaling. Typically used as a warm-up loop in practice sessions.

Roller: A small hill on a track; rollers are usually separated at regular intervals.

Wheelie: A trick in which the rider lifts the front wheel into the air while pedaling and maintaining balance.

Whoops: Another term for rollers, or bumps.

Author's Note

Thanks so much for reading this book—I hope you loved it. (I know I loved writing it, almost as much as I love riding bikes. And that's a lot.)

I hope you stay in touch. You can do that by going online and checking out Shred-Girls.com. We have a whole community of rad real-life young girls who love to ride, training advice and videos from coaches, all the intel you need to get started riding, and—of course—the inside scoop on Lindsay, Jen, and Ali's next adventures!

Come visit!

Love,
Molly

Acknowledgments

I'd like to thank the real-life Shred Girls who've submitted interviews for Shred-Girls.com and who've inspired me (and Lindsay, Ali, and Jen) on a daily basis.

My Baby-Sitters Club–loving sister who tolerated me narrating outfits as a kid and encouraged me to embrace my love of a good makeover montage whenever possible. My ultimate sidekick.

Lindsay, my original Shred Girl, who got me out of my shell as a kid. My partner in crime, and the girl who taught me the value of female friendship.

My parents, who let this Shred Girl develop at her own pace and find her love of bikes in her own time (but who fostered an early love of bikes, even though I was a reluctant athlete!).

My charming husband, who is not a comic aficionado but who now has a ridiculous understanding of the genre thanks to my constant chatter about superhero plot points. (As a cycling coach, however, his skills advice was invaluable.)

My amazing crew of friends, who helped by offering advice and opinions when needed, and especially Robbie, who helped edit the first draft into something infinitely better than my initial attempt.

Rodale Kids and the awesome editors I've been lucky enough to work with—especially Mark Weinstein, who first reached out; the amazing Trisha de Guzman, who has been a tireless editor and fellow secret nerd and bookworm to bounce ideas off; plus editors Caroline Abbey and Dani Valladares, who really helped make the Shred Girls come to life and cleaned up my messes beautifully. And of course huge thanks to the fabulous designer Jeff Shake and the incredibly talented illustrator Violet Lemay, who I swear could see into my brain when she sketched out what Lindsay, Ali, and Jen would look like! Huge thanks to them for making Shred Girls become a reality—and a book series that will reach tons of young girls and potential cyclists!

About the Author

Molly Hurford is an author, a coach, and a lover of all things outdoors. She's a cyclist and runner, as well as a sports and nutrition writer. She runs the online publication *The Outdoor Edit* and, with her partner, hosts a podcast called *The Consummate Athlete*. Her mission is "to get girls and women to embrace wellness and adventure!" *Shred Girls: Lindsay's Joyride* is her middle-grade debut.

For more adventures—both in real life and in the books—make sure you check out Shred-Girls.com.